Ever After High™

Fairy's Got

Talent

Ever After High

EVER AFTER Royals!

Fairy's Got

Talent

A SCHOOL STORY

Suzanne Selfors

L B

LITTLE, BROWN BOOKS FOR YOUNG READERS
www.lbkids.co.uk

For Alexa and Alyssa, who
magically appeared in my life,
as if transported by fairy dust.

LITTLE, BROWN BOOKS FOR YOUNG READERS

First published in the United States in 2015 by Little, Brown and Company
This edition published in Great Britain in 2016 by Hodder and Stoughton

1 3 5 7 9 10 8 6 4 2

A CIP catalogue record for this book
is available from the British Library.

ISBN 978-0-34913-200-6

Printed and bound by CPI Group (UK) Ltd, Croydon, CR0 4YY

The paper and board used in this book are made
from wood from responsible sources.

MIX
Paper from
responsible sources
FSC® C104740

Little, Brown Books for Young Readers
An imprint of
Hachette Children's Group
Part of Hodder and Stoughton
Carmelite House
50 Victoria Embankment
London EC4Y 0DZ

An Hachette UK Company
www.hachette.co.uk

www.hachettechildrens.co.uk

Contents

♡

♡

Wings

and Things

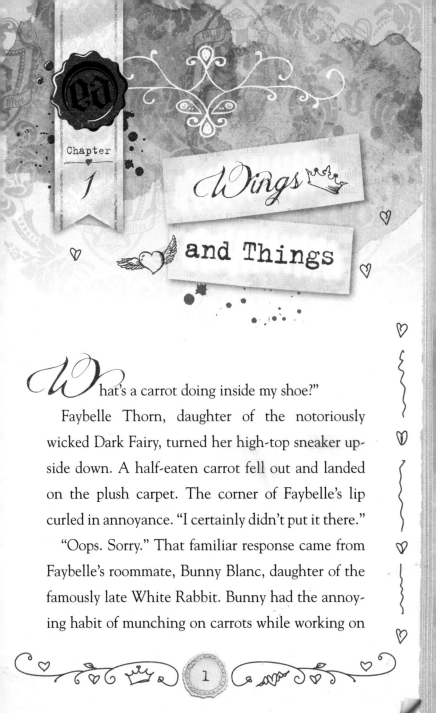

"What's a carrot doing inside my shoe?"

Faybelle Thorn, daughter of the notoriously wicked Dark Fairy, turned her high-top sneaker upside down. A half-eaten carrot fell out and landed on the plush carpet. The corner of Faybelle's lip curled in annoyance. "I certainly didn't put it there."

"Oops. Sorry." That familiar response came from Faybelle's roommate, Bunny Blanc, daughter of the famously late White Rabbit. Bunny had the annoying habit of munching on carrots while working on her thronework. Without looking up from her MirrorPad or her hextbook, she'd toss the carrot tops at the compost bin, but they'd often end up in other places. Yesterday Faybelle had found one in her sock drawer.

"I don't know how you can stand eating those things all the time," Faybelle said as she laced up her shoe.

"Carrots are delicious," Bunny told her. She collected the carrot top and dumped it into the bin. Then she grabbed her book bag and scurried toward the door.

"You know what I think is delicious?" Faybelle asked, a cool tone in her voice. Bunny stopped in her tracks and spun around.

"Turnips? Cabbage? Beanstalk roots?"

Faybelle raised a single eyebrow. "I think *dark magic* is delicious."

Bunny's eyes widened. Her gaze darted to the wall, to a painting of the Thorn family crest. In the center of the crest, the motto *Doers of Dark Magic*

wrapped around an evil-looking eye that seemed to follow Bunny no matter where she stood in the room. The painting was intimidating to some and inspirational to others, depending on what side of the magical world one stood. "You can't eat dark magic," Bunny said, though she didn't sound entirely convinced.

"A dark fairy can do whatever she pleases with dark magic," Faybelle coolly informed her.

Bunny's nose twitched. It thrilled Faybelle to see that her little "dark magic" comment had stirred uncertainty in her roommate. Of course, Faybelle would never use dark magic to *hurt* Bunny, or any other student at Ever After High. Causing harm to others could get her expelled. While at school, it was best to follow the headmaster's rules—or, at the very least, appear to be doing so. But every once in a while, a reminder was needed. Faybelle was no *ordinary* student. And that fact should never be forgotten—not by her roommate, not by anyone.

Faybelle's mother was the Dark Fairy, the one

who hadn't been invited to the celebration after Sleeping Beauty was born, and thus had cursed Sleeping Beauty to sleep for one hundred years. The Dark Fairy was royalty in the fairy world, and it was Faybelle's destiny to one day wear her mother's crown and become the most villainous of all fairies. It was, in Faybelle's opinion, a glorious destiny, and it filled her with pride.

So, as she looked at her Wonderland roommate, she smiled most wickedly. "In the future, I suggest you keep your veggie snacks on your side of the room." Her eyes blazed, and both beds rose off the floor, just a little reminder of her magical powers.

"Sure, okay." Bunny gulped. "You're right. I've been kind of messy. Oh dear, is that the correct time? I'm going to be late for a very important date." And off she went, as quickly as she could. Who could blame her for wanting to make her escape? Rooming with the daughter of the darkest of dark fairies was a bit unsettling at times.

Bark, bark.

Faybelle reached down and scooped a small fluff-ball into her arms. The creature was a wiggling, wagging, wet-nosed Pom-Pomeranian puppy named Spindle. These were the moments when Faybelle allowed her icy exterior to melt, for she loved Spindle with all her heart. This might have surprised some, but being a villain did not mean that Faybelle was incapable of love. Quite the opposite. Faybelle felt things deeply, and she loved her family with the ferocity of a fairy. Fairy hearts might be smaller than human hearts, but they beat with a rhythm that is powered by magic. Fairies are capable of love without measure.

But so, too, are they capable of the darker emotions, also without measure.

She kissed Spindle's head, hugged him, and laughed when he licked her cheeks. "That's enough, little one," she said tenderly. "I've got to finish getting dressed. It's a busy day, as usual." She set him on her bed. He stretched onto his tummy, watching while Faybelle finished tying her sneakers.

Shoes in place, Faybelle walked over to her vanity, carefully stepping over a turnip top along the way. Aside from Bunny's tedious habit of eating raw vegetables, there was nothing *wrong* with Bunny. But Faybelle couldn't understand why the headmaster had chosen such a weird pairing for roommates. Why not select someone who, at the very least, was part of Faybelle's story? Like Briar Beauty, who Faybelle would someday curse to fall into a deep sleep for a hundred years. Or, if not a character from her story, why not choose another villain's daughter, like Lizzie Hearts or Ginger Breadhouse? Or, even better, why not another fairy? At least a fairy wouldn't have a stupid collection of Wonderland teacups. A fairy wouldn't gnaw on roots and tubers! And a fairy would understand the importance of wing care.

If I ran this school, things would be totally different, Faybelle mused. She'd have an entire floor of the dormitory all to herself, as a future ruler rightfully deserves. Once she took her place as the Dark Fairy,

6

she'd come back to Ever After High and change things. *That will be a glorious day.*

But in the meantime, she had other things to tend to. Like her duties as the Cheerhexing Squad captain. Today was a very important day for her team. They would begin to learn a new routine for the regional tournament next month, where all the high schools in the fable districts would compete for the title of Cheerhexing Champions. Before Faybelle rose to the ranks of captain, the Ever After High cheerhexers had a losing streak that spanned generations. Faybelle was determined to bring home the golden trophy and place it in the trophy case in the Ever After High Grimmnasium.

Faybelle stood in front of her mirror. She pulled her shimmering blond hair into a high ponytail and chose a headband with a thorn ornament to hold her teal bangs in place. She inspected her reflection to make sure she hadn't forgotten anything. Her cheerhexing uniform included a shimmering skirt, a T-shirt with the letters *EAH*, and midnight-blue

leggings. The pom-poms were already tucked into her equipment bag. There was only one thing more to do.

She unfolded her wings.

Fairy wings are unique in the winged world. Neither made of feathers like a bird's wings nor stretched skin like a bat's, they are more akin to butterfly wings. Each wing is made of overlapping sections that are ultrathin. When light shines through, the sections act like prisms, casting brilliant colors and sometimes even rainbows. When not in use, the wings are folded and flattened against the back. Fairy clothing was tailored to include wing holes. Faybelle's wings were so iridescent they complemented any outfit she chose.

Faybelle glanced out the dormitory window. The morning was pleasantly sunny, the sky as blue as the icing on a thronecake. A perfect day for practice. She searched through the bottles, perfumes, and cosmetics on her vanity. She used many products to keep her wings healthy. After showering, she'd treat

them with a leave-on conditioner, to keep them glossy and supple. "Oh, there it is," she said as she grabbed a bottle. Then she reached over each shoulder and spritzed her wing tips with sunscreen.

"Always be proud of your wings," her mother had often told her. "They set you apart from the rest of the fairytale world. They are the symbol that you, my darling daughter, are *made* of magic."

I certainly am, Faybelle thought. With a satisfied smirk, she tucked Spindle in the crook of her arm and headed out to begin what she hoped would be another villainous day. And she made sure that her wings were proudly displayed for all to see.

A Fairy Fitting

It was during early childhood when Faybelle learned that her wings were all-important. Being raised in a fairy household, wings were a constant topic of conversation, the center of style, and the object of legends. There were paintings of wings and winged sculptures. Even their mailbox was shaped like a wing.

The mailbox stood at the end of the long driveway and read, THORN RESIDENCE. It contained the usual stuff—catalogs, bills, and junk mail. But it also

contained handwritten letters, mostly from young fairies, boys and girls, who hoped to one day meet the mailbox's owner, the Dark Fairy, aka Madame Thorn.

However, while the mailbox was stuffed to capacity, there was a certain type of correspondence that never appeared at the Thorn residence—invitations. Whether the event was a wedding, a birthday, or a reunion did not matter. It was the Dark Fairy's curse to never get invited to things. She went to a great deal of effort spying and eavesdropping, for it was important that she be seen at the most prestigious events. But if she stumbled upon a party in progress that had eluded her detection, she'd go into a rage. It made sense, then, that it was best to invite the Dark Fairy, so as not to feel her wrath. But whether they intended to invite her or not, everyone *forgot* to invite her. That was the curse.

Invitations were a sensitive subject in the Thorn household.

A guardhouse stood next to the mailbox, with a

goblin in attendance. It was his duty to inspect documents and identifications before allowing entrance through the silver gates. One might assume that the Dark Fairy's driveway would lead to an eerie residence—a gargoyle-infested fortress or a crumbling, bat-filled castle—especially because it was located in the Dark Forest. But the villa at the end of the driveway was of elegant design and built of white stone. Marble steps led to a pair of French doors, flanked on either side by tall windows that sparkled in the sunlight. A perfectly manicured lawn, sculpted hedges, and a shimmering koi pond lent an air of sophistication and impeccable taste.

The Dark Fairy herself did not look as one might expect, either. She did not shroud herself in midnight black or blood red, nor did she wear a mask or a cape. She kept no spiders, snakes, or rats at her beck and call, nor did she slink among shadows. Her floor-to-ceiling portrait graced the wall opposite the main entry. In this painting, her white hair was swept to the side, exposing a long pale neck. Her

dress was white silk with pearl buttons, and her heels were formed from elvish crystal. She looked the purest example of couture elegance. And upon her folded hands perched a single ring bearing the Thorn family crest. At first glance, one might think that her lack of embellishment was a sign that she was simple. But the painter had captured the truth in her dark eyes—she was an intelligent, complex being who knew the power of destiny.

Behind the portrait, up the winding staircase, third door on the right, was Faybelle's childhood room. This was a happy place, cluttered with stuffed animals, building blocks, crayons and paper—all manner of things to keep Faybelle busy, for she had been an active, quick-witted child who hadn't cared for idle time. Her personal understanding of wings occurred three days after her sixth birthday, when she was getting dressed in her room. But she was having trouble. "It doesn't fit!" she complained, her voice muffled by the pink shirt she was trying to yank over her head.

Her chambermaid, a mouse-sized fairy named Lucille, flew around Faybelle's waist, then tugged on the shirt's hem. The shirt wouldn't budge. "Your wings are in the way," Lucille declared.

"My wings?" Faybelle took off the shirt, then turned sideways and looked in a mirror. Sure enough, while she'd slept, her baby wings had tripled in size. She nearly burst with happiness. "They're so pretty! My wings grew! They grew!" Unaccustomed to the new size, she unfurled them without warning, accidentally knocking tiny Lucille across the room. Then Faybelle flapped her wings and rose right up to the ceiling. "Wow! Look what I can do!"

After ricocheting off the wall, Lucille landed face-first on a stuffed unicorn. She scrambled to her feet and shook a finger at Faybelle. "You come down here this instant, young lady."

Faybelle did. But she flew right back up. Up and down, up and down, laughing the whole time. Her baby wings had never lifted her more than a few inches off the ground. "I can't wait to show Mother."

"Well, you can't show anyone until you get dressed." Using a miniature pair of scissors, Lucille enlarged the wing holes in Faybelle's shirt. It still didn't fit perfectly, but at least her wings were comfortable.

"Hurry up!" Faybelle said, wiggling while the chambermaid selected a pair of shoes. "Won't Mother be surprised?"

"Madame already knows that your wings have grown," Lucille told her.

"How does she know?" Faybelle had only been out of bed for a short time. She hadn't yet seen her mother.

"Because the entire household can hear you shouting," Lucille told her. "You shouldn't shout."

"But my wings grew!"

While Faybelle danced around the room, Lucille flew after her, doing her best to brush Faybelle's messy white-blond hair. "Dear oh dear, you are a handful." She zipped around Faybelle's head, trying to get the locks to settle into place. But each time

she'd smooth a section of hair, Faybelle would spin around and mess the whole thing up. With an exasperated sigh, Lucille pushed Faybelle toward the door. "Out you go." Then she escorted Faybelle downstairs, through the grand entry, and onto the circular driveway, where the Thorn family's driver was waiting by a black stretch limousine. Its hood ornament was a pair of wings.

"Good morning, Miss Thorn," he said with a tip of his cap. His wings were as black as his suit, but the tips looked as if they'd been dipped in liquid silver. He opened the limo's back door. "Are you ready for an adventure?"

"Are we going somewhere? Aren't we flying?" Faybelle asked. "I can fly high now. My wings grew. Wanna see?" She lifted off the ground, higher than she'd expected. The sensation startled her, and she squeaked with alarm. The driver reached up and gently grabbed her ankle.

"I am impressed," he told her as he pulled her back to the ground. "But we won't be flying today,

because the weather is questionable. We wouldn't want you and your new wings to get caught in a rainstorm."

"Where are we going?" Faybelle asked.

"That is a surprise," Lucille told her. She gently pushed Faybelle into the limousine's backseat. But she didn't join her.

"Aren't you coming with me?" Faybelle asked.

Lucille hovered outside the car's door, her minuscule wings beating the air. "Madame will accompany you today," she said.

Faybelle gasped. Whatever they were doing, it had to be super important if her mother was coming along. No suitcases had been packed, so they must not be going far. But the Dark Fairy rarely went on errands, and Faybelle hadn't been told to dress for one of those parties where they always showed up uninvited. She squirmed, watching out the window for her mother to appear.

A few minutes later, the Dark Fairy flew out of the villa. She wore an elegant silver suit. Her white

hair was tucked beneath a pillbox hat. "Hello, darling," she said as she slid into the limousine and settled next to her daughter.

"Mother!" Faybelle wrapped her arms around the Dark Fairy and took a deep breath. The delicate scent of roses wafted from the nape of her mother's neck. It was a well-chosen scent, for though roses smell sweet, they also have thorns.

The driver closed the door. Lucille waved goodbye as the limousine made its way down the long driveway. Faybelle stopped hugging her mother, then pressed her face against the limousine's window. "Where are we going?" she asked. She waved to the goblin guard as he opened the gate.

"Your wings have begun to grow," the Dark Fairy said with a proud glint in her eye. "And they will keep growing until you reach adulthood. Therefore, the time has come for you to meet my tailor. From this moment forth, he will customize all your clothing to fit your wings perfectly."

New clothes? Faybelle scowled. That didn't sound like an adventure. "Couldn't we go to the Beast Garden? Or go get rainbow cones?"

Madame Thorn took her daughter's hand and stared into her equally dark, equally complex eyes. "This is important," she said. "Trust me."

The journey to Fairy Town took an hour, during which Faybelle wiggled and squirmed like a captive caterpillar in a jar. But finally, the colorful buildings rose into view. The driver turned down Main Street, passing shops and cafés. Sidewalks bustled with both winged and nonwinged individuals. Some carried packages, some walked dogs. Others gazed at window displays. Because of the large fairy population, there was additional traffic in the air and extra seating on the roofs for those who wanted to sip nectar with a breathtaking view.

The limousine pulled to the curb and stopped. When the driver opened the back door, Faybelle darted out and stood on the sidewalk. No one paid

much attention to her. A pair of fairies flew around her. A man with a phoenix on his shoulder didn't even bat an eye. A lady nearly bumped into Faybelle with her baby carriage. *Am I invisible?* Faybelle thought. *Don't they see that my wings grew?* She flicked them. Once. Twice. *Look at me.*

Suddenly, everyone stopped walking. Stopped talking. And all eyes turned and stared. But they weren't looking at Faybelle's wings.

The Dark Fairy had emerged from the limousine.

Her height was impressive, even more so in her crystal stilettos. She smoothed the wrinkles from her skirt and made sure her hat was perfectly in place. Then, with her chin high, she unfurled her wings. A collective "Oooh" filled the street. They were magnificent wings, powerful and delicate at the same time. As translucent as glass, but with black edging as if they'd been drawn in the air with a marker. For a moment, the rainclouds parted. The Dark Fairy turned slightly, allowing her wings to catch the sunlight. A rainbow fell across the limousine.

20

"Aaahh," the crowd said.

Those standing closest bowed their heads. "Madame," they whispered.

Then the Dark Fairy bent down and whispered in her daughter's ear. "Follow me. Hold your head high and do not make eye contact with anyone. Let them stare at *you*. Let them admire *you*." The gawkers stepped back as the Dark Fairy's wings began to flap. She rose a few inches off the ground, then flew toward a shop. Faybelle followed. She did her best not to look at anyone, but there was so much to see. There was a leprechaun with a Mohawk. A lady with goat ears. And that phoenix was adorable!

The Dark Fairy stopped outside a shop. A sign hung above the door.

FAIRY FASHION AND FINERY

The driver hurried forward and opened the shop's door, but at that exact moment, another fairy exited the shop. She was roundish in shape, wearing a simple cotton dress and casual shoes. Her blue hair was up in

a bun. Her wings were blue at the tips, but they were folded. She'd chosen to *walk* out of the shop.

"Oh, pardon me," she said with a little gasp, her hand flying to her chest as she nearly bumped into the Dark Fairy. Then she curtsied. "It is an honor to see you again, Madame."

The Dark Fairy said nothing. But her gaze could have melted stone. The blue-haired fairy stepped aside, making room as the Dark Fairy flew into the store. Faybelle then noticed a little girl who was holding the fairy's hand. The girl also had blue hair. Their eyes met. The little girl smiled. Faybelle smiled back. They were the same height. Maybe even the same age.

"My wings grew," Faybelle told her.

The blue-haired girl nodded. "Mine did, too."

"Faybelle!" the Dark Fairy called sternly. Faybelle darted inside.

The Fairy Fashion and Finery store was warm and quiet. There were no other customers, just a man with a pointed silver beard who'd been writing in a

ledger. But when he turned around and saw the Dark Fairy hovering in his shop, he dropped his feather pen. Then he bowed. "Madame, to what do we owe this unexpected…pleasure?" His hands began to tremble.

"It is time for my daughter's first fitting," the Dark Fairy told him. She flew to a leather chair, then sat. She folded her hands on her lap. "Well?" she asked with a hint of irritation.

"Yes, yes, of course." The tailor grabbed a measuring tape. "The daughter of Madame Thorn is always welcome in my humble shop. It is an honor to serve you." He didn't look honored. His legs shook and his face had gone a bit blotchy. As his fingers fumbled, he dropped the tape. "I do apologize for my clumsiness," he mumbled.

Faybelle didn't like having to stand perfectly still and be measured. She didn't much care about the fabrics or the type of thread, or whether buttons or zippers were selected. However, she did enjoy all the attention she was getting as townsfolk stood outside

the window, whispering and watching the proceedings. For a moment, Faybelle felt famous. But then she wondered, what was the blue-haired girl going to do next? Would she visit the Beast Garden? Or get a rainbow cone?

"Her new garments will be ready tomorrow. Shall I have them delivered?" the tailor asked.

"Of course," the Dark Fairy said. Then she waved her hand. A puff of fairy dust appeared, and three gold coins soared through the air and landed on the tailor's counter. "Good day."

The tailor hurried to the door, opened it, then bowed as she flew past. "Thank you for your patronage, Madame," he said. The crowd parted as the Dark Fairy and her daughter flew back to their limousine. Some bowed, some curtsied, while others dropped to their knees.

"Who was that fairy with the blue hair?" Faybelle asked once they were driving back up Main Street.

"Her name is Mrs. Goodfairy, and she is of no importance," the Dark Fairy replied.

This didn't make sense to Faybelle. "But she's a fairy. You told me that fairies are the *most important* beings."

The Dark Fairy gently pushed a loose strand of hair from Faybelle's forehead. "Yes, it is true that fairies are extra special because fairies are made of magic. The fairy with the blue hair is a fairy godmother. She has limited abilities. But we, my darling daughter, are dark fairies, and we wield unlimited power. Which is why we are the most admired *and* the most feared."

Feared? Faybelle realized the look she'd seen in the tailor's eyes, and in everyone's eyes when looking at her mother. It had been fear.

"Why are we feared?"

"Because, my dear, while fairy godmothers are servants to their magic, we dark fairies serve *no one*."

And that was the day when Faybelle Thorn learned exactly who she was, and who she was expected to become.

Pyramid Practice

Faybelle dropped Spindle off at the school's creature day-care center. Even though he was a very happy, well-behaved puppy, she couldn't keep an eye on him *and* on her team at the same time. Her goal was to mold the Ever After High cheerhexers into champions, but it wouldn't be easy. They still needed lots of guidance. So she didn't want any cute, tail-wagging distractions.

"Bye," she said after planting a kiss on the top of Spindle's head. "Have fun." She set him onto the woodchip-covered floor. He scampered away to join a hedgehog and a baby bear in a game of chase. Faybelle watched for a moment to make sure he was okay, then headed outside for practice.

She timed her arrival so that she would swoop in exactly five minutes late. It was important to make a grand entrance, but it was also important that *they* waited for *her* and not the other way around. She flew toward the field, the tips of her sneakers skimming the grass. Then she landed next to a pile of pom-poms. "Listen up," she said to a group of six fairies.

The six fairies had joined the Cheerhexing Squad after Faybelle became captain. And though these fairies were notoriously hot-tempered and feisty, they were the reason why the team was growing in popularity and why they had a good chance of winning regionals. Flying in formation was an awe-inspiring move, bringing the crowd to their feet every time. If Faybelle had her way, the Cheerhexing Squad would consist *exclusively* of fairies so that all cheers could be conducted in midair. But, unfortunately, there were

three wingless members on the team, which meant they had to do land-based cheers as well. Too bad.

The fairies flew into a frenzy as Faybelle approached.

"Faybelle, Faybelle, she's the one!"

"She's the one who makes cheerhexing fun!"

"Get out of my way!"

"I saw her first!"

"Quit pushing!"

"You quit pushing!"

Like lemmings, the six gathered around their leader, ready to follow her anywhere. They were Faybelle's minions. Having grown up in Fairy Town, they were in awe of her. This awe was partially real, but it was also keen strategy. They knew that by being in Faybelle's favor *now*, they stood a better chance of being in her favor when she became the next Dark Fairy. As the Dark Fairy's friends, they would become part of the fairy elite.

"Faybelle, you look glam."

"Adore your nail polish."

"I adore her nail polish more."

"You're just saying that because she likes me better."

"Want me to *spell* it out for you? I'm her favorite!"

When tempers flared, and they often did among these six, a hailstorm of spells could erupt, resulting in tails growing from backsides, hair catching fire, and pustules sprouting on noses. The constant bickering annoyed Faybelle, but having them fight for her attention was also satisfying. *Let them grovel. That's what minions are supposed to do.*

Faybelle raised a hand to silence them. They drew closer together, waiting for their captain to speak. "Where's the rest of the team?"

"There," a fairy said, pointing. Four students were hurriedly walking toward the field—a buff boy with brown hair, a tall girl with extremely long auburn hair, a petite girl with flaxen hair, and a winged girl with blue hair.

Upon spotting the blue-haired girl, the six sneered in the exact same way. "Farrah," they whispered with disdain. For if there was one thing they could agree on, aside from showing loyalty to Faybelle, it

was that they disliked Farrah Goodfairy, daughter of the fairy godmother from Cinderella's story. Faybelle joined them in the sneer. Farrah chose to *walk* alongside her friends, lowering herself to their ground level. Where was her fairy pride?

And to make matters worse, Farrah had befriended a new student at school, Meeshell, daughter of the Little Mermaid. Not only did Meeshell lack wings, but she also practically turned into a fish when she was in water. A fish!

"Hi," Farrah called with a wave.

"You're all late," Faybelle said, hands on hips.

"Sorry," Hunter told her. "It's my fault. I ripped my shirt." Hunter was the son of the Huntsman, and being one of the most muscular guys on campus, he tended to wear out his shirts quite often. "But Farrah fixed it." He pointed to his biceps. The shirt had been mended with shiny blue thread.

"I didn't use magic," Farrah said with a smile. "I used real thread, so it's a permanent fix. It won't change back at midnight."

"You're so talented," Nina Thumbell, the flaxen-haired girl, told her.

Faybelle rolled her eyes. Fairy godmothers did one thing and one thing only—they "make dreams come true," as Farrah liked to say. Which was totally lame. They couldn't conjure black magic, or cast evil spells. They could only make things look better, like turning a ratty dress into a ball gown, or transforming a pumpkin into a carriage. It was superficial magic and nothing, in Faybelle's opinion, to boast about.

And it only lasted until the last stroke of midnight. *What a joke!*

"Okay, listen up," Faybelle said, clapping her hands to get everyone's attention. "It's time to get started. We only have four weeks until regionals, so I expect everyone to be here on time, ready to work. Today we're going to learn a new pyramid formation. We're going to do an *inverted* pyramid."

"Inverted? But I thought Headmaster Grimm didn't want us doing any kind of pyramid," Holly O'Hair pointed out. From one look, it was obvious that Holly

was the daughter of Rapunzel. Her hair reached past her knees. Sometimes the other cheerhexers got entangled in it. "Pyramids can be dangerous."

"You're scared," one of the six fairies said. "You're afraid of heights."

"Can you blame me?" Holly asked. "My destiny is to be locked in a tower. Heights aren't exactly my favorite thing."

"You know, I also remember the headmaster saying we shouldn't do pyramids," Nina said. The daughter of Thumbelina, Nina was a good head shorter than everyone else. As the smallest member of the team, she was the most afraid of being crushed.

Faybelle glowered. She didn't like being questioned. It was true that the last inverted pyramid they'd attempted had been a royal fairy fail. She hadn't overestimated Hunter's strength. He'd simply gotten distracted when his girlfriend, Ashlynn Ella, walked by, and he'd ended up at the bottom of a heap of cheerhexers. There'd been bruises, sprains, and scraped knees and elbows. And six angry fairies

tossing spells at one another. The headmaster had also been walking past at the time, and he'd been concerned about having to explain injuries to their parents. "Keep it safe," he'd told them.

Faybelle tapped her foot, the way an annoyed cat taps its tail. Headmaster Grimm was always getting in the way with his rules. "I haven't received written notice that an inverted pyramid is forbidden. Have any of you?"

Holly shrugged. "No, but—"

"Then the decision is mine. As your captain, I say we try it again. If we're going to win regionals, we have to master the inverted pyramid." She raised an eyebrow, daring them to question her decision. No one said a thing. Faybelle smiled with satisfaction. "Hexcellent. Then, let's get started."

She flapped her wings and was about to lead her team onto the field, when a voice called out.

"Hi, everyone!"

"What now?" Faybelle grumbled. She turned to find Justine Dancer hurrying toward them, clipboard in hand. Justine was the daughter of the twelfth

Dancing Princess. Justine had long dancer's legs and wavy black hair. Faybelle winced as Justine's crown caught a blinding ray of sunlight. The wingless world had so many queens and kings, princes and princesses, it seemed as if half the population at Ever After High were royalty, destined for thrones. But in the fairy world, there was only one who ruled. Only one who commanded the fealty of all fairies.

"Hey, can I talk to you?" Justine asked.

"We're in the middle of practice," Faybelle said snippily. She hovered a few feet in the air.

"I just wanted to give you one of these." Justine pulled a flyer from her clipboard. "I wrote a play for Theater Club. I'm going to direct and choreograph."

"Writer, director, *and* choreographer?" Hunter asked. "Wow, that's impressive."

"Congratulations," Farrah said.

Justine blushed. "Thanks."

Faybelle landed in the grass, then stood face-to-face with Justine. "Did you run all the way out here for some sort of purpose? Or did you just want to tell us how amazing you are?" The six fairies snickered.

Justine stepped back. "Uh…" She swallowed nervously. She knew, as did everyone in the fairytale world, that it was never a good idea to annoy a fairy. "I came out here because I'm holding auditions. You don't have to be a member of the Theater Club. We'd love some new talent."

Faybelle read the poster:

✦ ONCE UPON A SPELL ✦

An original fairytale written, directed, and choreographed by Justine Dancer

Produced by Ever After High's Theater Club

OPEN AUDITIONS:

Saturday at noon in the Charmitorium

Sign-up sheets posted on the Charmitorium door.

"Auditions?" Faybelle folded her arms. "Are you joking? My cheerhexers are athletes, not actors. Besides, they're way too busy to be in a play."

"I'm not," one of the six fairies said.

Faybelle shot her a look. "As I said, they're way too busy."

"What about you?" Justine asked.

"Me?" Faybelle smoothed her skirt. "My schedule is wicked packed. I have a full course load with General Villainy, History of Evil Spells, Magicology, and Home Evilnomics. I'm on the Royal Debate Team, I'm president of the Villain Club, and I'm captain of this team. I'm up to my wing tips in activities."

"Yeah, up to her wing tips."

"You tell her, Faybelle."

"Faybelle, Faybelle, she's the one. She's up to her wing tips, and that's no fun!"

Even if she had a gap in her schedule, Faybelle thought acting was a ridiculous waste of time. Why bother? Actors didn't end up leading kingdoms.

How could being in some stupid play possibly help her future evil career?

But Farrah, Hunter, Holly, and Nina had gathered around the flyer.

"I've never acted in a play," Farrah said. "But I'd love to work on costumes. I can turn rags into silk, and plastic beads into pearls. I'm pretty handy that way. And if you want the costumes to last past midnight, I also know how to sew by hand." She pointed to Hunter's shirt.

"That sounds great but, actually, I was hoping you'd audition," Justine told her. "You see, I need someone who can fly for real."

"Why for real?" Hunter asked. "Can't one of your actors just put on a pair of wings and look like a fairy?"

A collective snort arose from Faybelle and her six fairies. "Dream on," Faybelle said. "I don't care if your actor has won the Golden Goblin Award. Fake wings will not make a human look like a real fairy. After all, we're *made* of magic." She and her fairies smiled wickedly, releasing little *poofs* of fairy dust from their fingertips like miniature fireworks.

Holly and Hunter sneezed. Nina wiped fairy dust from her eyes. Justine blocked the dust with her clipboard. "Under normal circumstances, anyone could audition for the fairy role," Justine explained. "But Headmaster Grimm said I can't use ropes to mimic flying." The fairy dust settled, and she lowered the clipboard. "I guess they did a play called *Escape of the Golden Goose* a few years ago, and the lead got tangled up in the ropes, flew into the audience, and fell right on top of Professor Rumpelstiltskin." She cringed. "So I either cut the flight scenes from my play or I find someone who can fly for the part. I don't want to cut the scenes."

"As I said, we're too busy," Faybelle told her. She was growing tired of all this talk about Justine's play. What a waste of time.

"You sure you won't audition?" Justine asked Farrah. "You could do costumes, too, if you wanted. I'd love to find a fairy for the role."

"Well…" Farrah touched the tip of her nose as she considered the plea. It was a gesture she did quite often, one that some found adorable but Faybelle found annoying as hex. "Perhaps I could do both."

Justine squealed with delight. She started to hug Farrah but stopped midway. "Oh, before you agree, I should probably tell you, the role's for a fairy queen. A *wicked* fairy queen. Would you be okay with that?"

Faybelle's skin prickled. "What did you just say?" She rose a few feet in the air. "Did you say a *wicked* fairy queen?"

"Yes. She's not the leading role, but she's super important to the plot."

Hunter nudged Farrah with his elbow. "Go for it," he encouraged. "It's good to do something unhexpected. I mean, look at me. I was trained to track animals in the woods and to rescue damsels. When I told my friends I was going to try out for cheerhexing, they teased me. But as it turns out, I really like being on this team. Except that time when the pyramid collapsed."

"Yeah, go for it," Holly said, putting an arm around Farrah's shoulders.

"You'll be great," Nina added.

Great? Anger made its way from Faybelle's toes to her wing tips. She wouldn't have been surprised if steam had shot out of her ears. A future fairy godmother was incapable of acting villainous. Farrah was a meek little Goodfairy. Giving her the part of the wicked fairy queen would be like telling a kitten to become a lion.

"Okay, you convinced me," Farrah said with a giggle. Faybelle watched with disbelief as the little Goodfairy signed her name to Justine's audition sheet. "I'll give it a try."

Faybelle Thorn knew what she had to do. She didn't have to *give it a try*. The wicked fairy queen was the role she'd been born to play.

"Move out of the way," she ordered, pushing between Farrah and Justine. Then she grabbed the pen and signed her name to the audition sheet. She

made sure she wrote in bigger letters. And with swirlier swirls. And an exclamation mark.

Farrah Goodfairy

Faybelle Thorn!

"I thought you were too busy," Justine said with surprise.

"I'm—I'm never too busy to help a fellow student," Faybelle said with a deceptive smile. "If you need a real fairy, then a real fairy you shall have." Then she turned to Farrah. "May the best fairy win." The words were so sticky sweet she could barely get them out of her mouth.

Justine tucked her clipboard under her arm. "Thanks so much. Remember, auditions are this Saturday at noon in the Charmitorium. Good luck. Or, as we say in the theater, break a leg!" And off she went.

"Yes, break a leg," Faybelle said to Farrah.

The six fairies snickered. "Or a wing."

"Yeah, break a wing."

"Hee-hee-ha-ha-ha."

Faybelle knew that landing this role was the chance of a lifetime. Playing the wicked fairy queen in front of the entire Ever After High community would send a very clear message—Faybelle Thorn was the real deal, no doubt about it. The *only* deal.

"Come on, team," she said. "Let's go kick some crown!"

The six fairies chanted as they followed.

Stomp (stomp, stomp), *stomp your feet!*
Ever After High (clap) *can't be beat!*

The Cheer

Factor

$\mathcal{M}$agicology class was taught by one of the most mysterious professors on campus, an elderly woman named Madam Baba Yaga. She was the department head for all classes having to do with spells, hexes, and general witchery. Whether you called her a witch or a sorceress, she looked like a combination of both. Her long gray hair was snarled and matted, and decorated with tiny bird bones. Her fingernails were chipped and as gray as ashes. But she didn't wear a pointed hat or a black cape. Rather, she

preferred a gypsy look, with bangle earrings and fringed scarves. And she traveled by pillow, which she insisted was more comfortable than a broomstick and easier on her old joints.

Madam Baba Yaga held student conferences and staff meetings in her office, which was one of the most unique rooms on campus because it never stayed in one place. Whether this was the result of Madam Baba Yaga wishing to challenge her visitors or the office itself growing bored and wanting new scenery was not quite clear. But throughout the day, the office would raise itself onto giant yellow chicken legs and rush around until it found a new location. Thus, meeting with the professor was always a chore. Which totally annoyed Faybelle.

Fortunately, the Magicology curriculum included lots of experimentation, and that required a larger room, so it was taught in a laboratory that never changed location. A footbridge over a moat, three flights of stairs, and two hallways were all that was required of the students to get to class.

It was a grand room with tall windows, stone archways, and walls lined with bookshelves. Lab tables were set up on one side, with rows of chairs on the other side for lectures. Magicology was reserved for students who could wield magic—the sons and daughters of witches, warlocks, sorcerers, and, of course, fairies.

Faybelle and her six fairy cheerhexers were the first to arrive. They claimed the front row, as they always did. Being in the front row meant the rest of the class could see Faybelle, even if it was just the back of her head. But nonetheless, her presence was known, unlike those who chose to sit quietly in the back row, wanting to go unnoticed. Like Raven Queen, daughter of the Evil Queen.

Without turning around, Faybelle was aware of Raven's presence. Fairy senses are finely tuned instruments. Raven used the same shampoo every day—Moonlight Essence. The moment Faybelle detected the scent, she knew her nemesis was near.

There was no reason for Faybelle to feel

threatened by Raven's presence in Magicology. Though destined for villainy, Raven refused to embrace dark magic. But in the past, when she'd tried her hand at good magic, the spells had almost always backfired. Her magic skills had improved slightly in recent months, but they still couldn't rival Faybelle's. It served her right, Faybelle believed, for denying her evil side. Raven was a rebel who didn't want her destiny. Faybelle shivered with disdain. She could barely stand to be in the same room with that traitor!

"Hi, Raven." Farrah Goodfairy's voice drifted from the back row. Why was she sitting next to Raven? They made such an odd pairing, but that was what happened at Ever After High. Friendships formed because some students chose to go off book. Faybelle shivered again.

"Good morning, students." Madam Baba Yaga floated into the room. She sat cross-legged on her magic pillow. A yellow scarf was draped over her head, and her peasant blouse had embroidered

sleeves. The pillow carried her to the front of the classroom, then lowered her to eye level. "Class is now in session. Please put away all MirrorPhones, MirrorPads, and any other nonmagical apparatuses, and focus your attention on the contents of this box in my hands." As she opened the box, dozens of tea-cups drifted out, then landed on her desk. Some were cracked, some chipped, some missing handles. "The cleaning fairies have asked us to help with a project, so we shall put our magic skills to good use this afternoon by fixing these teacups."

The cleaning fairies were among the smallest of fairies, about the size of a person's thumb. They flitted around the campus with their tiny feather dusters, brooms, and mops, leaving trails of fairy dust in their wake.

No one had to ask Madam Baba Yaga why there were so many broken teacups. "Stupid Wonderlandians," Faybelle mumbled under her breath. Just like her roommate, Bunny, the Wonderland students were insane about tea. In fact, one of their favorite sayings was *tea-riffic*. Because they drank it all the time, the Castleteria now stocked teacups, as did all the coffee carts around campus. Those darn things were practically everywhere.

"I'm afraid I couldn't quite hear your comment," Madam Baba Yaga said, looking directly at Faybelle.

Faybelle cleared her throat. "I was wondering, Madam Baba Yaga, why you want us to fix teacups. Isn't this a waste of our time? I mean, why not just get new ones?"

The other six cheerhexers nodded. "Yeah."

"That's right."

"Uh-huh."

"You go, girl."

Madam Baba Yaga pressed her fingertips together in a thoughtful manner. "I understand your concern for time management, Ms. Thorn. But while this may seem to be trivial work, no magic is trivial. Working with small pieces of porcelain will teach you control and patience."

"And it's recycling," Ginger Breadhouse pointed out.

"As Nina always says, it's good to recycle." Faybelle frowned at the sound of Ginger's voice. She was another rebel who didn't want to accept her villainous destiny.

"I love fixing things," Farrah said, her voice bubbling with enthusiasm. "This will be fun."

Faybelle raised her hand. "I'm wondering, Professor, is the teacup considered *fixed* if the spell wears off at midnight? Shouldn't that be considered a fairy fail?"

"It is not your place to concern yourself with another student's grades," Madam Baba Yaga said. Faybelle *humph*ed and slumped in her chair.

"For this assignment, you will use wands." Madam Baba Yaga floated over to the supply closet and pulled out a handful of wands. Then she tossed them into the air. Each wand flew directly to a student. Faybelle didn't need a wand. Fairies could use their fingertips as conduits for magic. But because she wanted a top grade in Magicology, she grabbed the wand. Madam Baba Yaga then distributed the broken cups so that each student had a small pile on his or her desk.

"I can't believe I'm fixing teacup chips," Faybelle grumbled. She tapped a cracked green cup with her wand and said, "Crack be gone, fix that cup." The porcelain regrew inside the crack, and the cup looked good as new. *So easy!* Laughter erupted in the very back of the room. A few students had gathered around Farrah's desk. Three of her teacups had been fixed and were dancing around her desk.

Ginger, however, wasn't having much luck. One by one, her teacups jumped onto the floor, then scuttled from the room. "Come back here!" she called. She pointed her wand. One of the cups morphed into a cupcake. "I'm much better at cooking spells," Ginger said in frustration.

Faybelle looked at the remaining pile on her desk. She had four more cups. And two were covered in dozens of cracks and chips. It would take forever to fix all the little imperfections. However, there was a time-saving method she could use. Faybelle smiled wickedly, for she had a special talent. She could take any spell and make it more powerful with a cheerhex. She called

this the Cheer Factor. So she stepped away from the table, pulled her pom-poms from her bag, and cheered.

> *Fix them up.* (rustle, rustle)
> *Fix them up.* (rustle, rustle)
> *Cracks begone.* (stomp, stomp)
> *Fix these cups.* (stomp, stomp)

With a proud smirk, Faybelle set her pom-poms aside and watched her spell take root. Fairy dust swirled around the cups as the porcelain began to regrow. But then the cheerhex took an unexpected turn. Even after the cracks had been filled, the porcelain kept growing, and growing. Each cup swelled, then exploded.

"Eek!" Ginger cried as a storm of porcelain shards flew at her. She covered her face as they landed on her pink dress. Their sharp edges tore the fabric like tiny claws.

Faybelle narrowed her eyes. That wasn't the result she'd expected. But then again, a shower of sharp teacup shards could be considered evil. She might get hextra credit.

"Are you okay?" Raven asked.

"Yes, but…" Ginger held up her hand. "I pricked my finger." She looked nervously at Faybelle. Everyone looked at Faybelle.

Raven stepped forward. "Faybelle, did you do that on purpose? You know it's not Ginger's destiny to prick her finger."

"Are you really going to lecture *me* about destiny?" Faybelle's snort was echoed by her minions. "I know all about destiny. I embrace it. You threw yours away." Raven winced as if Faybelle's words had stung. Was there some lingering guilt? Some questions about her choices?

A single drop of blood ran down Ginger's finger. "Am I going to fall into a hundred years' sleep?" she asked worriedly. "I can't go to sleep. I have a test tomorrow in Cooking Class-ic, and I have a new episode of my MirrorCast show to record."

"Don't get your pink head in a tizzy," Faybelle said with a dismissive wave. "I didn't curse you."

Ginger let out a big sigh of relief. Madam Baba

Yaga located a bandage in one of the many first-aid kits. Accidents were plentiful in Magicology.

Farrah hurried to Ginger's side. "I can't heal your finger, but I can fix your dress if you'd like."

Ginger's face lit up. "Yes, would you, please?"

Farrah looked to Madam Baba Yaga for permission. She nodded. Farrah waved her wand in the air. A little musical sound emerged, and a trail of fairy dust swooped around Ginger. In the blink of an eye, Ginger's dress was lovely again. "As good as new," Farrah said. "Until midnight, that is."

"Thanks," Ginger said. "You're so helpful."

"I make dreams come true," Farrah told her. "It's what I do."

"'It's what I do,'" Faybelle mimicked under her breath.

While the other students finished their assignment, Madam Baba Yaga handed Faybelle a dust broom and instructed her to sweep up the mess. The six cheerhexers began to fight over the broom.

"I'll do it!"

"No, let me!"

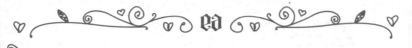

"I want to help Faybelle!"

"No, I do!"

"Stop kicking me!"

"Only if you stop kicking me!"

"Can't we just call the cleaning fairies?" Faybelle asked.

"There is a wise old saying," Madam Baba Yaga said. "'She who cleans up her own mess learns to not make it the next time.'" With a flick of her wrist, the dust broom landed in Faybelle's hand. Then she floated around the room, checking on everyone else's progress.

As Faybelle swept up the shards, she tried to hide her frustration. Her attempt to impress everyone had failed. But at least Raven hadn't impressed them, either. Just as the dismissal bell rang, Faybelle dumped the shards into the garbage. She grabbed her equipment bag and was about to leave, when Madam Baba Yaga called her name.

"Ms. Thorn. A word with you."

A Bit of Advice

s the classroom cleared, Faybelle's shoulders stiffened. She'd never been asked to stay after class.

"Yes, Professor?" Faybelle didn't smile sweetly or bat her lashes. She didn't need to fake politeness. A villain was a villain, and Madam Baba Yaga would never try to change that. There were some who considered her to be a villain, since she was a daughter of the darker forces. But Faybelle had never witnessed villainous behavior from the elderly professor. Strict behavior, certainly, but never evil.

Madam Baba Yaga slid off her magic cushion and stood in front of Faybelle. Though diminutive in stature and a bit crooked in the spine, she revealed her vitality in her eyes and voice. "It is apparent to me that you are not fond of Ms. Queen."

"Well, that's putting it mildly," Faybelle said. "I detest her. Raven is a rebel, and she ruined her story."

"What makes you believe that Ms. Queen has only one story?"

"What do you mean?"

"Our stories contain many chapters, Ms. Thorn. Cursing Sleeping Beauty was just one chapter in your mother's life. You, for example, are another chapter. Do you see my point?"

"No."

Madam Baba Yaga sighed. Her scarf slipped from her head, but she did not adjust it. Instead, she looked deep into Faybelle's eyes. "Ms. Queen is not your rival."

"She should be," Faybelle said. "She should be doing everything she can to be a villain. But she turned her back on her story. I won't do that. I will

curse Briar Beauty, and it will be a glorious moment in fairytale history! I'm proud of my story."

"But you want more than your story, don't you? You want to expand your destiny. That's the real reason why you see Ms. Queen as your rival."

Faybelle said nothing. *What the hex?* Was the professor a mind reader?

"Ms. Queen's refusal to become the next Evil Queen leaves a broken link in a powerful chain," Madam Baba Yaga said. "I am not judging you, Ms. Thorn. It is natural for a villain to want absolute power. You are following your instincts, and that is what we expect."

"If Raven doesn't want to be the next Evil Queen, then someone has to take her place," Faybelle said. "Why not me?"

Madam Baba Yaga nodded. "Your passion is admirable. There are many at this school who are giving up on their wicked heritage." She walked to her desk and sat in the carved chair. "And Ms. Good-fairy. What is your problem with her?"

Faybelle adjusted her ponytail. "Oh, she's just annoying. All that goody-goody stuff, all day long. 'I'll fix this, I'll fix that.' Everyone thinks her magic is so wonderful, but all she does is make things look better. That's not significant magic. It's not even powerful. How can an entire career be built on magic that only lasts until midnight? I don't get it. But everyone *loves* her."

"And you want that love?"

"No, of course not." Faybelle rolled her eyes. "I'm a villain. I don't need *love*."

To Faybelle's relief, the professor didn't push the conversation. Faybelle looked at her MirrorPhone. She needed to get some thronework done before dinner. How much longer was she expected to hang out?

Madam Baba Yaga opened a ledger and grabbed a quill. Faybelle leaned closer, watching while the professor wrote two capital *F*'s next to Faybelle's name. "What in Ever After? Why'd I get a fairy fail?"

"You did not complete today's class assignment."

"But, Madam, I only broke teacups. And when you think about it, they were already broken."

The professor wrote an A next to Farrah's name. "The assignment was to *fix* the cups."

Faybelle stomped her foot. "But this is so unfair. My shards tore Ginger's dress. That's a very wicked thing to do. I should get some kind of credit for being wicked."

"But you were not wicked on purpose, were you?"

Faybelle considered saying she'd ruined Ginger's dress on purpose, but there was no use in lying. Madam Baba Yaga had the unnerving ability to detect deception.

"While your work today was disappointing, you show a good deal of potential, Ms. Thorn. You have discovered that you possess a special kind of magic. Many of my students go years before they figure out their own magical touches. You can use a cheer to increase the potency of your magic. I find that most intriguing."

"Then can I have hextra credit? To offset the fairy fail?" Faybelle watched, hoping the professor would make a new mark in the ledger.

"No, I think not. You used your magic touch unwisely. Today you only broke teacups. But tomorrow who knows what could happen if you are not more careful? You must hone your skills. You must proceed slowly."

"I don't want to go slowly. It's soooo boring. And besides, I don't have the time. I have a zillion things to get done."

Madam Baba Yaga set aside her quill, folded her hands once again, and looked into Faybelle's eyes. "Faybelle Thorn, your impatience could be your downfall. Listen to me very carefully. Those who are destined to wield great power, be it evil or good, must be the most careful of all."

Faybelle smiled. "You think I'm destined to wield great power?"

"If you so choose."

"I do choose. I do!"

"Then have fortitude, Ms. Thorn. Don't rush the process. Your magic will grow as you grow. It will mature as you mature. You scared Ms. Breadhouse today. And some other students, too."

"They should be scared of me," Faybelle said proudly. She puffed out her chest. "They should *all* be scared of me. I'm a villain!"

"Yes, but this was not a good show of your skill. It did not make them respect you. Dark magic only brings respect if it's done well. An unnecessary evil spell is a waste of magic and talent." She picked up her quill again. "That is all. Good day, Ms. Thorn."

Bag in hand, Faybelle flew from the classroom. Despite today's fairy fail, Madam Baba Yaga had told Faybelle that she was destined for greatness. At that moment, Faybelle felt as if she could fly all the way to the moon!

A Perky Prediction

fter leaving Magicology, Faybelle headed toward the creature day-care center to pick up Spindle. Out on the quad, a group of students stood beneath a giant mirror screen, their heads tilted upward, their eyes wide with anticipation. Mirror screens hung all over campus—on walls, on tree trunks—but they were not provided so students could check their hair or makeup, though Daring Charming always used them for this purpose. The mirror screens were for school-wide communication.

Headmaster Grimm used them to deliver his constant announcements. And Blondie Lockes used the screens to broadcast her MirrorCast show, *Just Right*, a daily dose of journalism, gossip, and commentary about the deeds, doings, goings-on, and goings-wrong at Ever After High. Blondie's show was what the students were eagerly awaiting.

Blondie's smiling face appeared in the center of the mirror screen. Her blond curls bounced as she talked. Her baby-blue eyes were practically electric. She possessed the kind of energy that always sent a chill of revulsion down Faybelle's spine. Perkiness. That was what it was. Pure, undiluted perkiness. Blondie practically bubbled over with the stuff. But though Blondie was an annoying chatter bug, Faybelle stopped to listen. Blondie was always in the know, and that was an enviable talent.

"Hello, fellow fairytales," Blondie said. "It's time for a brand-new edition of *Just Right!*" Theme music began to play. "As usual, I have the latest scoop on what's happening at Ever After High." The theme music faded.

"On this very day, both Faybelle Thorn and Farrah Goodfairy signed up to audition for the role of the wicked fairy queen in the Theater Club's upcoming play. According to my sources, neither Farrah nor Faybelle has any acting experience, so this should be interesting. Here to discuss the situation is Justine Dancer, the play's director, writer, and choreographer."

It wasn't unusual for Faybelle to be mentioned on Blondie's show. There'd been a report about her selection as cheerhexing captain, another report about her campaign and election as Villain Club president, and a string of reports about the time she'd competed for the title (and should have won) Next Top Villain. Even though she still needed to get Spindle and she had a ton of thronework, she decided to stick around and watch the show for a few minutes. Blondie always had an opinion. And if Justine was favoring someone for the role, Blondie would get her to admit it.

The camera shot widened to make room for Justine. She and Blondie sat side by side. They both had so many waves and curls their hair filled the entire screen. Blondie didn't waste a second. "Tell us, Justine, who do you think will make a better wicked fairy queen? Faybelle or Farrah?"

"I don't know," Justine said with a shrug. "My decision will be based on their auditions."

"But doesn't it seem to you that Faybelle was made for the part? She's perfectly wicked. She has *evil* in her blood. I've seen her lose her temper, and she can be downright *dangerous*."

A couple of students who'd been standing next to Faybelle sidestepped, creating a wide berth between themselves and the *evil*-blooded fairy.

Blondie held the microphone closer to Justine. "The very nature of acting is to pretend to be someone different from oneself," Justine explained. "Often, it's more difficult to play a part that's similar to who you really are."

That's ridiculous, Faybelle thought. Because her blood coursed with evil DNA, playing the wicked fairy queen would be super easy. But Farrah was way too sweet. So sweet she was probably made of candy, not magic!

"Well, I still think it would be fun to take a poll of the students." Blondie looked into the camera. "What do you think, fellow fairytales? Will Faybelle or Farrah prove to be the better actor and get the part? Hext me right now."

All the students in the quad pulled out their Mirror-Phones and began hexting. Faybelle didn't bother. She felt a bit uneasy. If this was a popularity contest, Farrah might stand a chance at winning, but only because she was a Goody Two-Wings. If the students really thought about it, really weighed the options of a silly future fairy godmother versus a malevolent future dark fairy, then there'd be no contest.

Justine held up her clipboard. "There's still room on the audition sheet, so if anyone watching would like to try out, please add your name. The sheet will be posted outside the Charmitorium. Auditions are this Saturday. Along with the wicked fairy queen, we'll need actors to play the forgetful prince, the

melancholy princess, the elderly king, and a family of trolls. We'll also need singers for chorus members and dancers for the dance troupe."

"Oh, the hexts are coming in," Blondie reported as she read from her own MirrorPhone. "From early results, I can tell you that Farrah Goodfairy is definitely favored to win the role."

"That doesn't matter to me," Justine said, shrugging. "My decision will be based on the actual audition."

"Well, you heard it here. Farrah is favored to win." Blondie leaned so close to the camera you could count her freckles. "Thanks for watching. I'll see you next time with the latest scoop. Remember, if it's not too hot or too cold, it's *Just Right*." The mirror screen went dark.

Everyone turned and stared at Faybelle. Her wings stiffened. She felt her cheeks go red. "What are you do-gooders looking at?" she snarled. "You know I'm made for that part!" Then she flew off in a huff. Blondie's prediction would not come to pass. She couldn't read the future. She wasn't even magical!

At the creature day-care center, Faybelle collected Spindle. The little puppy was tuckered out. Though the hedgehog had rolled himself into a ball, the baby bear had proved to be as rambunctious as Spindle, and they'd chased each other for hours. Faybelle gently set him into the puppy carrier and was about to leave when Farrah entered the center.

"Hi, Faybelle," she said, but she didn't smile in her usual way. She looked a bit sheepish. "Uh, did you watch Blondie's show?"

Faybelle said nothing.

"Don't pay any attention to that nonsense," Farrah said. "It doesn't matter what the student body thinks. It's up to Justine. And I'm sure you're a much better actor than I am." She reached into the sawdust-filled pen. A little mouse climbed onto her hand. "Clydesdale loves coming here. There are so many critters to play with." She stroked the mouse's ears. "Your puppy is very cute."

Faybelle continued to give her a cold shoulder.

Why was Farrah being so friendly? Didn't this girl know anything about competition?

"Have you chosen your monologue?" Farrah asked.

This question surprised Faybelle so much she broke her silence. "My what?"

"Your monologue. You know, for the audition. You have to memorize it."

"I'm supposed to *memorize* something?" If there was one thing Faybelle hated, it was the feeling of being left out—left out of parties, of course, but equally distressing was being left out of information. "I thought we just showed up and read from the script."

"Oh no, you're supposed to have a two-minute monologue prepared. You have to memorize it *and* perform it."

Faybelle clenched her hand around the puppy carrier's handle. She squeezed so hard her hand began to ache. This was preposterous. She had a zillion things to do that week. She had to perfect

the pyramid and write a new cheer, plus there was a research paper for History of Evil Spells, a speech for the Villain Club, and all her daily thronework. Besides, why should she have to work for this role? It should be handed to her on a silver platter.

"I don't know how Justine expects me to find time," Faybelle said. "Does she think I'll just conjure a time-expanding spell? She knows that's against the rules!"

"I can help you." Farrah's blue eyes sparkled. "I'd be very happy to help." The little mouse squeaked as if he wanted to help, too. They were both so happy and cute that it turned Faybelle's stomach.

"Why would you do that?" Faybelle asked, raising an eyebrow suspiciously. "We're competing against each other." She would never help a competing cheerhexer. Never ever after! This Goodfairy clearly had cotton candy between her ears. That notion gave Faybelle an idea. Her speech for Villain Club could be called "How Being Full of Goodness Impairs One's Intelligence"!

"I don't think of us as competitors," Farrah replied with a sincere smile. "Besides, it's all friendly, right?"

Faybelle almost laughed out loud. The words *friendly* and *competitors* had no right to be in the same sentence. Competition existed for one thing only—victory. Winners ruled, losers drooled. No one ever said the opposite.

"I don't need your help," Faybelle said. "I'm perfectly capable of doing this on my own. I *never* need help." Snoring arose. Spindle had fallen asleep, exhausted from his playdates. Faybelle tucked the puppy carrier under her arm and zipped out of the room. Imagine that. A Goodfairy wanting to help a dark fairy. Didn't anyone in this school know her place?

But as Faybelle rounded the corner, a thought filled her mind—an idea as brilliant and sparkly as fairy dust. Practicing her audition with Farrah would be the perfect way for Faybelle to check out her competition. And that would be so much easier than sending the cheerhexers to spy. They always got distracted or ended up bickering. If Faybelle

wanted to get something done correctly, she knew it was best to do it herself.

She turned around and flew back into the creature day-care center. Farrah was setting her mouse into a tiny carrier. "On second thought," Faybelle said, "I do have a bit of time right now. If you *insist*."

"Oh, that's great news. How about we go to my room? I have a book on monologues that I checked out from the library." She picked up her tiny carrier and whispered through the little window, "What do you think about that, Clydesdale? We're going to have guests." The mouse squeaked again.

Faybelle Thorn, daughter of the Dark Fairy, was on her way to the room of a Goodfairy. Life at Ever After High was certainly full of surprises.

Light

and Dark

There'd been a time, in her younger years, when Faybelle hadn't cared whether her friends were descended from evil bloodlines. She'd just wanted to have fun. If you lived in Fairy Town and you received a notice to send your offspring to a playdate at the Dark Fairy's villa, you *did not* refuse. All sorts of children filled Faybelle's summers with laughter and games. But one in particular was her favorite.

It was the summer before kingdergarten, and Ginger Breadhouse, daughter of the Candy Witch, visited

once a week. The first time they met, Faybelle was speechless. She stared, openmouthed, at the strange woman who was holding the little girl's hand.

Lucille, the chambermaid, flew around Faybelle's head, then whispered in her ear, "She's a witch."

Ginger's mother was not *just* a witch—she was a wicked witch. And she looked the part, with her matted green hair, pointed black hat, ragged black dress, and battered military boots.

The Dark Fairy greeted her guests. "Faybelle, darling, I'd like you to meet the Candy Witch and her adorable daughter, Ginger."

"Hello, dearie," the witch said. She leaned close to Faybelle. "Would you prefer to be baked or fricasseed?" Faybelle gulped. "I'm kidding, of course." The witch cackled. "It's a joke. A joke."

"My mom doesn't eat kids," Ginger said with a smile. She had bright pink hair that was pulled into two pigtails. "She never ate Hansel or Gretel. That's just a mean thing people say about her." Ginger held out a plate of cookies. "These are for you."

Faybelle peered at the doughy lumps. "Are those cookies *humming?*" she asked.

"Yep." Ginger giggled. "They're made with singing sprinkles."

"Wow!" Faybelle reached for one, but the Dark Fairy gently blocked her hand.

"I don't mean to insult you but, by any chance, are those cookies poisoned?" the Dark Fairy asked the witch.

"Poisoned?" She burst into a fit of cackling. "Of course not. I would never try to poison a comrade's daughter."

Faybelle turned and looked at Lucille, who was hovering beside her ear. "Comrade?" Faybelle whispered.

"They are comrades because they are both villains," Lucille whispered in return.

"Go on, girls. Go play while the Candy Witch and I visit," the Dark Fairy said. "But don't bother the goblin guards. And don't go near the dragon. He hasn't been fed yet."

With squeals of delight, each girl grabbed a cookie and ran outside. Faybelle ate her cookie in two bites. Ginger put an ear to Faybelle's tummy. "It's still humming," she said. They both fell over laughing.

Those summer days were lovely and carefree. Rolling in the grass, leapfrogging through the gardens, splashing in the koi pond. Ginger always brought new, unpoisoned treats, like massive macaroons, spelly doughnuts, and cinnamon trolls. It was childhood at its best.

One evening, after a day of playing with Ginger, Faybelle sat at the long dining table with her mother. Faybelle's cheeks were rosy from the sun, and her little wings were tired. "Mother?" she asked as she stuck her spoon into a bowl of fairyberry sherbet. "Why don't you look like a villain?"

"What do you mean?" the Dark Fairy asked.

"I mean, Ginger's mom looks like a witch. And the sorcerer at the end of the street looks like a sorcerer. But you don't wear black capes or black hats. You don't wear black at all."

"How delightfully observant of you." The Dark Fairy sat back in her chair and smiled approvingly at her daughter. "Black is used in stories to represent dark forces—this is true—while light is used in stories to represent goodness. But light isn't good or bad. Light has no moral compass. Light is power. Light is energy. And magic is the manipulation of energy." Her diamond necklace twinkled beneath the chandelier. Her pearl-white dress radiated. Her pale skin glowed as if she were a living lightbulb.

Faybelle didn't completely understand, but she knew that her mother's message was important.

The Dark Fairy took another sip, then continued. "Why should we, the darkest of fairies, shroud ourselves in black capes and black hats? Why should we cling to the night?" She pointed a finger at Faybelle's bowl. A puff of fairy dust shot out, and a perfect swirl of whipped cream appeared on Faybelle's sherbet.

"Embrace the light," the Dark Fairy said. "Never, ever, live in the shadows."

Chapter 8

An Abundance of Blue

pparently, Farrah Goodfairy had so many wingless friends she'd gotten used to walking. There were times when it was necessary for all fairies to walk—when the doorway was too narrow, the ceiling too low, or the hall too crowded. But Faybelle didn't care if her wings knocked a few students off their feet. She always made a point of flying whenever she could. *Everyone else* should make room for her.

"Hi, Farrah."

"Hi, Cedar."

"How's it going, Farrah?"

"Hi, Melody. It's going great."

Farrah waved to passersby as if she were in a pageant. She greeted this student and that student. They wished her happiness and health. Pleasantries were exchanged. She smiled. They smiled. She laughed. They laughed. It was some kind of mutual-appreciation festival. Even her mouse squeaked his greetings.

Faybelle, however, elicited the opposite reaction. Most of the students glanced warily at her or darted aside to avoid her wings. *Well, I'm clearly not going to win a popularity contest*, she realized. Normally, Faybelle wouldn't give a twinkle about the Good-fairy's social status, but the undeniable truth that Farrah was beloved could hurt Faybelle's chances of being cast as the wicked fairy queen. Even though Justine had said she'd hold a fair audition, she'd definitely want the performances to be sold out. Farrah, with all her friends, would most likely draw a huge crowd. That fact alone could sway Justine's decision. Faybelle's eyes narrowed as she thought about all this.

Another reason to spy on Farrah and crush her chances!

Farrah Goodfairy's room was tidy and quaint. No carrot tops littered the floor. Or turnips. Or any other stupid root vegetable. She'd made no decorating choices that would be considered trendy or bold, which surprised Faybelle. She would have thought a fairy who focused on appearances so much would have a much louder room. But the simple decor sort of fit with Farrah's personality—sweet and friendly. There was a canopied bed, lots of soft pillows, and an overstuffed chair that looked very inviting. And the paint, bedspread, pillows, and wallpaper palette were all variations of one color.

"What's the deal with you and the color blue?" Faybelle asked.

"It's my favorite color," Farrah said. Then she pointed to her hair. "Can you blame me? Blue is with me all the time. I'm so lucky. Plus my roommate,

Meeshell, also loves blue. She says it reminds her of the ocean."

Of course the mermaid would like blue, Faybelle thought. She didn't admit that all the blue hues actually made her feel relaxed. If she had this room, she'd nap all the time, which would be fine if she were Briar Beauty, but not fine for a fairy who was trying to become the wickedest, vilest, darkest Dark Fairy ever after!

Faybelle stifled a yawn, and her gaze traveled across a vast corkboard. Unlike her own room, there was no family crest with the motto *Doers of Dark Magic*. Instead, Farrah had covered the corkboard with photos of friends. There she was, smiling with Apple White, taking a selfie with Ashlynn Ella, and posing with Blondie. And there she was with Justine, at a party that Faybelle hadn't been invited to since she was the daughter of the Dark Fairy, who never got invited to anything. And another photo of her and Justine at the Hocus Latte Café.

"You and Justine are *friends?*" Faybelle hissed.

"Sure. I'm friends with most everyone," Farrah said simply.

Faybelle spun around and glared at her competitor. "Oh, isn't that a delightful coincidence," she said, her voice dripping with insinuation. "You're auditioning for a play, and you just happen to be *friends* with the director."

"That won't matter," Farrah said, her cheeks reddening. "Justine will choose based on talent."

"Uh-huh. You expect me to believe that?" Faybelle pointed to another photo, and another. "You two apparently go to a lot of parties together. Did you see *me* at any of those parties?"

The ensuing silence was as thick as the Castleteria porridge. Farrah opened her mouth, then closed it. She clearly didn't know what to say. How could she admit that she'd gone to all those parties without hurting Faybelle's feelings? She was momentarily paralyzed by her niceness. *How pitiful.*

"Just so you know, I don't get invited to parties, because it's my curse. It's not because people dislike me."

"I'm sure it's not," Farrah said politely.

"The curse makes them *forget* to invite me. That's how it works. It's the same curse my mom has. That's why she wasn't invited to the celebration of Sleeping Beauty's birth. Got it?"

"Okay." Farrah nodded as if she understood. "I'm sorry you have that curse."

They stared at each other. The realization that Farrah felt sorry for her only made Faybelle more upset.

Spindle woke from his nap and started yapping. Faybelle placed the pet carrier onto the carpet, then set Spindle free. The puppy leaped out and immediately pounced on a sock, chewing it to bits.

"Don't worry about the sock," Farrah said. "I can always fix it later."

"Who said I was worried?" Faybelle darted over to Farrah's desk. It was piled high with books—utterly boring titles like:

101 Things You Can Do With a Pumpkin

How to Turn a Mouse into a House and Other Affordable Decorating Tips

From Rags to Riches: How to Make Her Look Like a Princess

Faybelle picked up a book with a well-worn cover and read its title. "*Does Everything Have to End at Midnight?* Why are you reading this?"

As Farrah set her mouse into his little mouse castle, she explained. "All fairy godmothers would like their spells to last longer, but we have to accept the midnight decree. Whenever I start to question this rule, I read this book, and it reminds me that midnight is part of my story and I should be grateful that I'm given the opportunity to help others, even if it's only temporary."

"Why don't you try to change the rule?"

"Change it?"

"Sure." Faybelle lowered her voice and whispered in an ominous way, "With *dark magic*."

"Oh no, I'd never do that." Farrah's gaze darted around. She looked like she wanted to run from the room. To run from the words themselves. *Dark magic*. "A Goodfairy shouldn't even *think* about dark magic. You know that."

A knock on the door broke the tension. "Farrah?" Apple White entered the room. "Oh, hello, Faybelle. How fairy, fairy odd to see you here." She walked up to Farrah and stuck out her right leg. "I'm going to dinner tonight with Daring, Darling, and Dexter, and my tights have a run. I called my dwarf network, but they can't get me a new pair until tomorrow. I'd be royally grateful if you'd—"

"Of course." Farrah flicked her wand. A few musical notes and some fairy dust drifted through the air, and—voilà—the tights were good as new.

"Thank you!" Apple squealed with delight. "I wish my story had a fairy godmother. You're the best. I owe you one." She hugged Farrah. Faybelle rolled her eyes. Why so much happiness? It was just a pair of tights. It's not as if Farrah had made any lasting impact on the world.

Faybelle told herself that the only reason Apple was fond of Farrah was because of the Goodfairy's ability to mend tights and do other menial things like that. But deep down Faybelle knew better.

Apple, like most of the students at Ever After High, truly *liked* Farrah because Farrah was nice. She cared. She helped. And if Faybelle hadn't been so over-scheduled *and* on a villain trajectory, she might have taken some time to hang out with Farrah.

Oh my godmother. Am I starting to like her, too?

Faybelle pushed that crazy thought from her head. "Don't you get tired of helping everyone?" she asked after Apple had left the room.

"Well, sometimes it's a bit tiring, I admit that." Farrah sat on her bed and slipped off her blue shoes. "But it's my duty and my destiny to help others. You know, I think that's why I'd like to be in this play. I'm always behind the scenes. I'm always the supporting role. It would be fun to be the star of the show, just one time. To be…important."

Behind the scenes? Faybelle tried to remember the details of Farrah's story. "You turn mice into horses, a rat into a coachman, and a pumpkin into a coach. That's very important." She couldn't hide her sarcasm. And she didn't try.

Farrah frowned. "I know you don't think my magic is significant, not compared with the kind of power you'll have. But sometimes being able to change the way something looks does more than simply change the surface. It's not just about making Apple *look* good. If she feels good, and she has confidence, then she feels empowered. That kind of attitude can change someone's destiny."

Faybelle leaned against the desk and folded her arms. "Changing someone's destiny is the talk of a rebel."

"I'm not..." Farrah straightened her back and held her head high. "It's my duty to serve others. That's what I do. And I'm proud to serve."

And it's my duty to serve no one.

But enough with the boring chitchat. "So, what about your monologue?"

"Oh right, the monologue." Farrah smiled. She hurried to her desk and grabbed a book. "I almost forgot. Have you read Shannon Pale's version of the Sleeping Beauty story?" Faybelle shook her head. "Well, it's very good, especially the scene where the

Dark Fairy bursts into the castle and confronts the king and queen. I chose that speech."

Faybelle clenched her jaw. Farrah Goodfairy was about to perform the part of the story that belonged to Faybelle's mother! Sure, it was a fictional version, written by a bestselling author, but it annoyed her to the core. "Go ahead," Faybelle said as she slowly sat on the edge of the desk. "Amaze me." It would, of course, be a disastrous performance. Farrah had no instinct for villainy.

Farrah cleared her throat. With the book in one hand, she unfurled her wings and lifted herself above the bed. "Your Majesties," she said, not in a sweet voice but in one that demanded attention. "Forgive my intrusion, but I couldn't help noticing that you are in the middle of a party. Did you forget to mail my invitation? Perhaps it was lost." Her brow furrowed, and her voice rose to a nearly thunderous level. "Surely you wouldn't purposefully leave me off the guest list. You wouldn't dare!" Spindle stopped chewing on the sock and dove under a pillow.

Faybelle could barely hide her surprise. The little Goodfairy was delivering the monologue like a pro. How had she conjured that powerful voice, the authoritative stance, the determination? One might think she'd been studying for years at a professional acting academy. If she was this good at the audition, there'd be a standing ovation for sure.

Any notion of liking or spending time with this Goodfairy disintegrated. This was a competition, and there could only be one winner. Somehow, some way, Faybelle had to stop Farrah from auditioning.

"Gotta go," Faybelle announced, interrupting the stellar performance.

"But—"

"It's getting late, and I have way too much to do." She tossed the pillow aside, scooped Spindle into her arms, then set him back inside the carrier.

Farrah gently landed on the carpet. "But what about *your* monologue? You haven't found one yet."

"I already found it. I'm going to do the same monologue as you." Faybelle grabbed the book from

Farrah's hand and took a photo of the page with her MirrorPhone.

But instead of acting concerned or accusing Faybelle of copying, Farrah just smiled. "Oh, that's a hexcellent idea," she said. "I think it will be fun if we both do the same monologue."

Of course she thought it would be fun, Faybelle thought. She didn't have a competitive bone in her body.

Which is why she is doomed to lose!

"See you at the audition," Farrah called as Faybelle hurried down the hall. "I hope I helped you."

Oh, you've no idea how much you helped, Faybelle thought.

The Vault

of Lost Tales

After dinner that evening, Faybelle flew to the Charmitorium. She wanted to make sure no one else would be auditioning for her coveted role. The audition sign-up sheet was tacked to the wall. Lots of students had added their names to the various roles, but only two names appeared for the wicked fairy queen—Farrah Goodfairy and Faybelle Thorn.

Hexcellent news. Even though Faybelle had a ton of thronework to do that night, she had to find the time for an additional project. Like a true dark fairy, she would remedy this situation with Farrah. If she could stop Farrah from auditioning, then the role of the wicked fairy queen would be hers. With Farrah out of the running, Faybelle wouldn't have to do anything but show up. She could recite some baby poem, like "Peter, Peter, Pumpkin Eater," and she'd still get the part.

But could she keep Farrah from auditioning? That was the all-important question.

Threats and blackmail came to mind. But while those were acceptable villain tactics, they were also traceable. She couldn't risk getting dungeon detention, not when she had so much on her schedule. She'd have to eliminate her competition in a different way.

She'd have to use dark magic.

Faybelle's mother had a favorite spell. She was fond of cursing those who displeased her. After sleeping for months, even years, on the front lawn, her victims would wake up, bleary-eyed and confused. This spell did wonders for instigating loyalty in her subjects. But it was well known, and if Faybelle employed it, there would be finger-pointing for sure. She'd have to find something subtle, something that wouldn't announce, "Dark magic at work."

While most of the student body lingered in the Castleteria, eating dessert and chatting about everything that had happened during the school day, Faybelle flew across campus to the one place that might provide her with an answer.

The Vault of Lost Tales was aptly named because it contained books that had long been forgotten. What better place to find a spell that no one would recognize? There was a time when the vault had been locked up tight, off-limits to most. But it was now open to students, though few chose to visit, not only because it was an eerie place, but also because the books within it weren't on any of the class lists. They'd been *forgotten*, after all.

The vault was located far beneath the school, through a labyrinth of dank hallways and tunnels.

There was no room to fly down there, so Faybelle hurried along the stone floor. For some, the vault was a treasure trove, a place to discover books that had been buried, thrown away, or simply abandoned. For most, it was a dusty, moldy, and cold room with creepy decor such as rat nests and bats. To make the place more unappealing was the rule that books discovered in the vault could not be checked out, for that would mean they'd been found and were no longer lost. So research had to be done within the vault itself.

As Faybelle entered, she inhaled a cobweb. "Gross," she muttered. "Somebody get some cleaning fairies down here."

Once she stopped coughing, she looked around. Every shelf and most every inch of the stone floor was stacked with books. She'd been using her flashlight app on her MirrorPhone to light the way. Because there was no electricity beneath the school, a bin filled with candles and matches sat at the entrance. Open flame did not seem wise when there

was so much paper about, but candlelight was tradition. Besides, it lent a mysterious glow to the place.

"Hello?" Faybelle called. The empty librarian's
desk had a brass nameplate.

GILES GRIMM, LIBRARIAN

He was probably at dinner, which is exactly what
she'd hoped. She didn't want anyone asking her reason for visiting.

The thing about lost books is that to remain lost,
they cannot be cataloged. So there were no index
cards to peruse, no database to search. It was a matter of walking the narrow aisles, looking and hoping
for something to catch the eye.

With a lit candle in one hand, she wound her way
around towering stacks and started with a shelf at
shoulder level. She eagerly ran her finger across
book spines, reading the titles one by one. *Mrs. Giant's
Diary. Healthy Meals for Trolls. Fun Facts about
Fangs.* How utterly disappointing. Nothing sounded
even remotely like dark magic.

Of course, she could call her mother and ask for help. But Faybelle wasn't a child any longer. She needed to solve her own problems. There was no pride in having one's mother come to the rescue. She was determined to fight her own battles. How proud the Dark Fairy would be when Faybelle succeeded!

The unmistakable sound of a page being turned caught Faybelle's ear. "Hello?" she called again. She hurried to the end of the aisle, then groaned with disgust. "What are *you* doing here?"

Raven Queen was sitting in the corner, wedged between two stacks of books. A long purple cloak was wrapped around her like a blanket. While the eerie vault did seem like the perfect place for a couple of future villains to hang out, Raven had proved that she wasn't villain material. So why was she here? Why wasn't she eating thronecakes in the Castleteria with everyone else?

"Oh, hi, Faybelle." She glanced up from a book she'd been reading. "Aren't you cold?"

"No." But in truth, Faybelle was nearly shivering.

Though her cheerhexing uniform did a good job wicking away sweat, it couldn't protect her from the chilly air that inhabited the vault.

Awkward silence ensued. They'd each journeyed to the bowels of Ever After High for a reason. Who would spill that reason first? It took about a minute for Faybelle to win the staring match.

"Uh, I found this interesting book," Raven said. "It's called *My Life as a Toad*. The author was a great-great-great-uncle of Hopper Croakington II's. After his spell wore off, he wrote about his adventures."

Faybelle was dumbfounded. "You're down here reading about a toad?"

"Well, actually, I came down here to see if I could find something about misfiring spells. But I got distracted." She closed the book and got to her feet. "I'm sure you've noticed that I sometimes have trouble with my good spells. I'm getting better, but I still need to practice."

"You don't have to come down here to find the answer. Everybody knows what's *wrong*."

"What do you mean?"

"News flash. You're not supposed to cast good spells. It goes against your destiny. It goes against your story. You don't need a book to tell you that." Faybelle pointed a finger. "Look in the mirror, Raven. You're the Evil Queen's daughter, and that's who you were meant to be. Not a *good* queen. An *evil* one. *The* evil one."

Raven pulled her cloak tighter. "I'm meant to be whomever I choose to be."

"Oh my godmother, more rebel talk." Faybelle wanted to plug her ears. It pained her to hear such things. "How can you be so…so…?"

"So what?"

"So ungrateful!" Faybelle shouted angrily. She spun on her sneakers and stomped away, turning down the next aisle. There was nothing more to say to Raven. They stood on opposite sides of a huge divide, but Faybelle knew that her side was the correct one.

Forget about her, Faybelle told herself. *I came here to find something important. Not to waste time thinking about Raven Queen.* She began to peruse the next shelf. More ridiculous titles. *Riddles about Rodents. How to Make a Court Jester Hat. Trolls Have Feelings, Too. Whatever after! Yeesh.* No wonder these books were lost and forgotten. Where was something about dark magic?

"You don't have to hate me."

"Huh?" Faybelle nearly jumped out of her tights. Raven had moved as silently as a shadow and was standing right next to her.

"You don't have to hate me just because I'm try-ing to choose a different path," Raven said.

A whole mess of emotions flooded Faybelle's head, and for a moment, she felt faint. Were they really going to have *this* conversation? Faybelle had already made her opinion perfectly clear. "What don't you get?" she asked. "Your mother and my mother are two of the most important, most powerful

women in fairytale history. You should be proud. You should *want* your destiny." Faybelle pushed a strand of white-blond hair from her eyes. "But you choose to be a *rebel*." How she hated even saying that word.

Raven remained calm. Her violet eyes didn't flash. Her jaw didn't clench. Nor did she avert her gaze, but rather, she looked directly and confidently at Faybelle. "I'm not ashamed of my destiny. I love my mother, as you love yours. But before you label me, ask yourself this…aren't we all rebels in some way? Don't you, Faybelle Thorn, have some desire to go off book?"

"Never!" Faybelle blurted. But as the word echoed off the ceiling, she knew it was a lie. If she extended the Dark Fairy's power and claimed the authority that once belonged to the Evil Queen, then she would be creating a new story.

"Then I guess you've got it all figured out." Raven looked at her MirrorPhone. "Well, I'd better get back. I still have thronework. I hope you find

whatever you're looking for." With a swish of her cloak, she turned and left the vault.

Good riddance.

Faybelle pushed the conversation from her mind. She had a matter to contend with that was much more important than Raven Queen's insinuations.

After a solid hour of fighting cobwebs, stirring up dust clouds, and shivering, Faybelle finally found something. Her heart skipped a beat as she pulled the book from its home on the shelf. It was a small book, the size of a wallet. The pages were crumbling and the binding had deteriorated so that the whole thing was being held together by a few stitches. *Forgotten Fairy Spells.*

She gasped. This was unbelievable. Exactly what she wanted. She sat on the nearest stack of books and carefully opened the cover. What an amazing find. The pages were handwritten in miniature letters. One of the diminutive fairies must have been the author. She held the candle close to the page, squinting to read. According to the introduction, these spells could only be cast by fairies and would only work on fairies. *Perfect!*

But then, as she turned the pages, her hopes withered. Most of the spells were illegible, stained with mold, or missing passages because of rot. But one spell, in the back of the book, had survived intact.

Wilted-Wing Spell
Wings of beauty, soft and bright,
droop and wilt and bring no flight.

Faybelle's wings twitched. Her fingers twitched, too. The instructions said that the victim of the spell wouldn't be able to fly until a full passing of the moon. One month. This was even better than she'd hoped. If Farrah's wings wilted, she wouldn't be able to fly. And Justine needed an actor who could fly.

And because this was a forgotten fairy spell, the school administration wouldn't recognize it. They'd think Farrah had some sort of illness that had caused her wings to wilt.

It was brilliant, and perfectly wicked.

Faybelle read and reread the spell until it was seared into memory. She tucked the book into a dark corner, behind a stack so it would remain forgotten. Then she ran out of the vault, her feet carrying her as swiftly as wings.

Things were about to get delightfully evil.

A Deed

Most Devious

The rest of the week passed quickly. Faybelle kept up with her various duties. She wrote her speech for Villain Club. It started out as "How Being Full of Goodness Impairs One's Intelligence" but that got complicated, so she changed it to "How Being Nice Makes You Stupid." She couldn't find any academic research to support this claim, so she used her own observations as examples. The speech got a standing ovation from her fellow villains.

She also wrote a new cheer for regionals.

Spell!
Say what? Say what?
Spell!
That's what we do!
We spell,
We spell for you!

There was some discussion among team members, since not all of them could cast spells, and they worried that the audience might think they were talking about spelling, as in spelling words. So Faybelle had the fairies release puffs of fairy dust at the end, to make it clear they were talking about magic. And even though they'd had a few tumbles, the inverted pyramid was coming along nicely.

In addition, Faybelle completed all her thronework assignments, took Spindle for daily walks, kept her wings in tip-top condition, and maintained an air of superiority. But all the while, she kept that forgotten wilted-wing spell in mind. She'd unleash it at the perfect moment. Farrah would be foiled. Poor little thing wouldn't know what hit her. But there was no reason to feel sorry for Farrah. In one month she'd be fine again. Back to normal. It's not like wilted wings would be such a big deal to her, because she *walked* most of the time. At least, that was what Faybelle told herself every time she tried to imagine what it might be like to have wilted wings.

Saturday finally arrived. Auditions were at noon.

"You look different," Bunny said. "Where's your uniform?"

"I can't wear a cheerhexing uniform for a theater audition. That would be idiotic." Faybelle stood in front of her full-length mirror. She'd chosen a white dress that was accented with tiny crystals. She'd also selected a pair of glittery shoes. When light hit her, she glowed.

"Light is power," her mother had often told her. "Never hide in the shadows."

"What about a hat?" Bunny was particularly fond

of a black top hat. "A hat is one of the most necessary accessories."

"A hat?" Faybelle scowled. Those Wonderlandians were always talking about tea and hats. Why would a queen wear a hat? Then she realized what was missing. "A crown! Of course." She opened the closet and searched the shelves until she found a tiara made of crystal thorns. She plopped it onto her head. The outfit was complete. She didn't thank Bunny for the suggestion. After all, a crown was *not* a hat. "Will you watch Spindle while I'm gone?"

"Sure," Bunny said. "I'll take him for a walk."

Faybelle handed the leash and a bag of treats to Bunny. Then she kissed Spindle's fluffy head. He wagged his tail and kissed her back.

"Break a leg," Bunny called as Faybelle flew from the room.

Nervous energy coursed through her, which was odd. Faybelle was used to performing in front of crowds. She'd given plenty of speeches and she'd led her cheerhexers countless times. But she was so jittery it felt as if actual pixies were trapped inside her stomach. Was that even possible? Had someone cast a spell on her? Of course not. She was being paranoid. It was normal to feel a bit nervous before using dark magic. At least, that was what she told herself.

Her plan was this—just before Farrah delivered her monologue, Faybelle would cast the spell. Unable to fly, Farrah would give up and Faybelle would swoop in and show Justine how a real wicked fairy queen commanded the stage. Then she'd call her mother and share the good news. The Dark Fairy would be so proud.

Students were milling outside the Charmitorium. Some were practicing monologues. Others were chatting. As soon as Faybelle landed on the steps, Blondie Lockes stuck a MirrorPad in her face. The red recording light was flashing. "Hi, Faybelle," she said. "I was hoping to get an interview before the audition. Did you know that most of my viewers are predicting a landslide win for Farrah?"

Faybelle glowered at the perky reporter. "This isn't an election. Who cares what your viewers think?" She flicked her wings, sending a gust of air right into Blondie's face.

Blondie coughed. "But do you agree with them? Do you think Farrah stands a better chance?"

"No comment." But as she fluttered up the steps, she realized that her coldness could draw suspicion later, when everyone was trying to figure out why Farrah's wings had wilted. So Faybelle turned back around. "Oh, Blondie!" she called with a little wave. Blondie held up the MirrorPad. "I wish Farrah the very best, and I know that Justine will be fair in her selection." It took every ounce of focus not to cringe after saying those words. What a load of Pegasus poop. She waved again and forced a smile. Wow, maybe she was a talented actor after all. Blondie smiled back.

It was crowded inside the lobby. But a chorus of familiar voices drew her attention.

"Faybelle!"

"There she is!"

"Faybelle, Faybelle, she's the one. She's the one who makes auditions fun!"

"Stop pushing me."

"You stop pushing me."

Her six cheerhexers shoved and elbowed their way around the other students until they were standing next to their captain. Each was sipping from a Hocus Latte cup. "For you," one of them said, handing Faybelle a mocha frappé, her favorite.

"You look amazing."

"Sooooo amazing."

"You deserve this part."

"You sooooo deserve this part."

"Stop mirroring me."

"You stop mirroring me!"

"Okay, enough," Faybelle said. She took a sip. Maybe the sweet beverage would settle her stomach. "Now, you know what you're supposed to do, right?" She'd given them specific instructions after practice yesterday.

"Yes, we're supposed to clap."

"Hextra loud."

"And cheer."

"When you're done with your audition."

"But we don't clap or cheer for anyone else."

"Only you."

Faybelle nodded. Having her own fan club was hextremely convenient. She checked her Mirror-Phone. It was almost noon. "Let's go, team." Like a flock of birds, they flew across the lobby. Students jumped out of the way.

"Whoa," Humphrey Dumpty called as he wobbled, nearly falling over.

The Charmitorium was one of the most impressive rooms at Ever After High. Hundreds of seats faced a gilded stage. The stage was graced by blue velvet curtains. There were plush box seats and dozens of golden chandeliers. Faybelle and her cheerhexers chose seats in the front row, center. Faybelle glanced around until she spotted Farrah, sitting next to Briar and Ashlynn, a few rows behind them. Farrah hadn't dressed like a

wicked queen. She looked as she always did, with her blue dress and blue hair. She waved. Faybelle forced herself to wave back. If the audition was based on appearance alone, Faybelle would definitely get the part. But alas, that was not how it worked.

There were other familiar faces as well, such as Dexter and Daring Charming. Farrah's roommate, Meeshell, was there, too, along with a bunch of students from the Glee Club. Humphrey hurried in, followed by some student dancers. Justine took the stage.

"Welcome, everyone," she said, clipboard in hand. Her denim jacket had DIRECTOR embroidered on the back. "Welcome to the auditions for *Once Upon a Spell*. If you're here for Fableous Flutes tryouts, they've been moved to room 201." A couple of kids with flutes scrambled out of their seats and left. Justine continued. "I speak for everyone in the Theater Club when I say we're hexcited to see so many new faces. I hope you're not nervous. We are all friends here, so please don't worry too much. There are lots of parts, and if you don't get a lead, I can find room for you in the chorus or on the dance team."

"We're all friends," Faybelle thought. She held back a snicker. *That's what you think.*

"So this is how we'll proceed. First we'll have auditions for the melancholy princess and the forgetful prince, the elderly king, and then for the wicked fairy queen. Then we'll take a break and audition for the remaining roles. Each actor will come up here and deliver a two-minute monologue. Callbacks will be next week."

"Callbacks?" Faybelle blurted.

Justine squinted. Faybelle's gown was glowing beneath the Charmitorium chandeliers. "There will be callbacks in case I can't make up my mind. I will narrow it down to two actors, and they will come back to audition a second time. There are lots of students auditioning, so I might have trouble deciding. For instance, there are ten girls trying out for the melancholy princess."

"Ten?" Faybelle grumbled, then sank low in her chair. This was going to take all day. She stretched her legs and rested her feet on the edge of the stage.

"Okay, let's begin," Justine said, reading from her clipboard. "First up is Briar Beauty."

Faybelle watched as, one by one, the actors took the stage. Briar was okay, but she kept yawning. Ashlynn was really good. Meeshell seemed a little nervous at first, but midway through her performance, she seemed to gain confidence and pulled off a good audition. "Who knew fish could act?" Faybelle whispered to the cheerhexer on her left, who hexted the comment to the other cheerhexers. They all giggled.

As the auditions continued, the cheerhexers paid no attention, hexting one another to pass the time. Faybelle went over the spell in her mind again and again.

Seven guys tried out for the part of the forgetful prince. Dexter Charming and Daring Charming both auditioned. Dexter, like Meeshell, lacked confidence, so his voice was hard to hear, but his performance didn't improve midway through. If anything, he seemed to get more nervous. Daring, however, strode all over the stage, blinding everyone with his smile. He was certain to get the lead. He even forgot his lines, which was perfect for the part. Humphrey Dumpty was the last to try out. Sure, he was a prince in real life, but Faybelle couldn't imagine him being cast as a leading man. He was a tech geek who was always tripping on stuff. He'd end up in the chorus, for sure.

"What an epic bore," Faybelle whispered under her breath.

"You're so right."

"Hextremely boring."

"Total torture."

"Fairy fail."

"Makes me want to go all Evil Queen."

"Get your elbow off my armrest!"

"Okay, next up, we have the role of the wicked fairy queen," Justine said. Faybelle sat up straight. She'd been so focused on her spell she hadn't even noticed that the tryouts for the elderly king had passed. "There are three names on the list, so we'll begin with—"

"Excuse me?" Faybelle leaped to her feet. "What do you mean, *three*? It's supposed to be just me and Farrah."

Justine read her clipboard again. "It looks like a new name was added this morning."

What the hex? Someone had dared add her name to the audition sheet? Who would do such a thing? Faybelle looked around the room, at each gilded chair, even up in the balcony. Her gaze landed on two fairies who were sitting in the back row. She didn't know them. They were first-years. Which one was auditioning? *Drat!* The spell was designed to wilt the wings of only one fairy. Now she'd have to eliminate *two* fairies. Her thoughts spun as she tried to figure out what to do. And then the perfect solution popped into her head.

She'd have to cheerhex the spell, to increase its potency. "Give me those," she said, grabbing a pair of pom-poms. "I gotta do something."

"We'll come with you," the cheerhexers said in unison.

"No, stay here," she hissed as she lifted into the air.

Justine shielded her eyes with her hand. "Faybelle? Where are you going? You're up first."

"Uh, I need to make an important call. Let Farrah go first. I'll be right back." And out the door she flew.

After landing in the lobby, Faybelle closed the Charmitorium doors behind her. Fortunately, the lobby was empty. Something else must have caught Blondie's attention because she wasn't hanging around, waiting for a scoop. There was no time to waste. Farrah would soon be on the stage, delivering her perfect monologue, proving to everyone that she could act. Pom-poms in hand, Faybelle cheered the spell.

> *Wings of beauty,* (rustle, rustle)
> *soft and bright,* (rustle, rustle)
> *droop and wilt* (stomp, stomp)
> *and bring no flight.* (stomp, stomp)

She aimed the fairy dust at the Charmitorium. The dust swirled, then disappeared through the crack beneath the door. She lowered her pom-poms and took a long breath. The devious deed was done. There was no going back. If regret, worry, or guilt tickled her conscience, it was too late. She'd cast dark magic at a fellow student.

It shouldn't take too long. A fairy would notice immediately if her wings—

A heart-wrenching cry arose from inside the Charmitorium.

Wilted

Wings

*F*aybelle tossed the pom-poms aside. She didn't want anything to arouse suspicion. When she stepped back into the Charmitorium, she would prove to everyone that she was, without a doubt, a natural-born performer. She would astonish them all with her ability to act as if she knew *absolutely nothing* about Farrah's wilted wings.

She opened the doors. "What in Ever After is going on?" she asked as innocently as possible. "Did something happen while I was on my MirrorPhone?"

She batted her lashes and put her hand to her heart, as if concerned. Oh, she was good.

Farrah stood alone onstage, all color drained from her face. "My—my—my wings," she stammered. She spun around. "They won't unfurl." She spun again, her long blue hair twirling with her. "What's wrong with them? This has never happened." A strangled whimper escaped her lips. "I don't understand. I—I—" She turned and looked imploringly at Faybelle. "What's wrong with me?"

Faybelle shrugged. "How should I know? I wasn't anywhere near you when this happened." She said this loudly so everyone in the Charmitorium could hear. "You're not accusing me of anything, are you?" She clenched her jaw, ready to defend herself if necessary. If magic was suspected, she'd point to the other fairies in the room. They were as capable of casting a spell as she was.

"No, of course not." Farrah's eyes seemed as wide as tea saucers. "But my wings aren't working. Do you know what it could be? Has this ever happened to you?"

Poor, misguided creature. She wasn't accusing Faybelle. She was looking to her for advice.

Faybelle flew onto the stage and stood next to the little Goodfairy. It was the perfect opportunity to showcase her superior physical attributes. She took her time strutting around Farrah, pretending to inspect Farrah's wings. But in truth she was giving Justine time to observe the difference between the two fairies. *I'm taller, stronger, and much more regal,* Faybelle thought. *The choice is obvious. I'm your wicked fairy queen.*

"My, my, this is a mystery," Faybelle said, feigning confusion as she touched one of the limp wings. The sight of the stricken appendages was indeed shocking. For a moment, Faybelle's chest felt a little heavy. She wondered if she'd done the right thing. But then she pushed that thought from her mind. She made some *tsk-tsk* sounds. "I have no idea why your wings are just hanging there. It's so unattractive. My wings *always* work." To prove her point, she lifted off the stage and soared over the audience, skimming

their heads. Ashlynn and Briar ducked. Humphrey fell out of his chair. The cheerhexers cheered.

"Faybelle!"

"Faybelle, Faybelle, she can fly!"

"She can fly up to the…Hey, watch your elbow!"

"You watch your elbow!"

Faybelle landed back onstage. Farrah was visibly trembling, her eyes filling with tears. A lump formed in Faybelle's throat. What was going on? Was she feeling bad for this Goodfairy? *No, never! A dark fairy does not feel bad about casting dark magic!*

Justine hurried onto the stage. "I'm so sorry this has happened," she said, wrapping her arm around Farrah's shoulder. "Do you think you'll get better if you take a break? Or go get a drink of water?"

"I could try," Farrah said. "But fairies never lose the ability to fly. Unless they are hextremely ill." Gasps arose in the audience.

"She's right," Faybelle said. "Hextremely ill."

"I'm sorry to disappoint you," Farrah told Justine. "You said you needed someone who can fly, and if I

can't fly, I can't audition for the wicked fairy queen. But you still have two others who are trying out."

"That's right," Faybelle said. She zipped around them, then hovered. "My wings are just fine. But I don't know about the other—"

A shriek erupted from the back row. Then another. Faybelle could barely contain her smirk.

"What's going on?" Justine called.

The two first-year fairies had leaped from their seats. "My wings!" one of them cried. "Something's wrong with my wings."

"My wings, too."

They struggled down the row, pushing past other students until they burst into the aisle. Then they spun around, trying to unfurl their wings, but both sets hung limp and lifeless.

Well, this is going exactly as planned, Faybelle thought. She rubbed her hands together in a most satisfied way. Then she opened her mouth, about to tell Justine she was ready for her monologue, when her six cheerhexers also jumped from their seats.

They didn't cheer. They shrieked and wailed as they also discovered useless wings.

"Faybelle!" they cried. "Faybelle, what's happening?"

Holy hex! She'd been in such a hurry to foil Farrah and the other auditioning fairy she'd forgotten that the spell would attack *every* fairy in the room. Panic welled in her chest. Her heart began to pound. Her wings beat in double time as she continued to hover. How could she have made such a rookie mistake? This would be a huge problem for the Cheerhexing Squad. Regionals were three weeks away, but the wilted-wing spell was supposed to last for an entire moon cycle! How could they fly in formation?

She'd sabotaged her own team!

The weight of what she'd done pressed down on her shoulders, pushing her until she was standing on the stage.

"Oh, you poor dears," Farrah said. She hurried off the stage and ran up the aisle. "Oh dear, oh dear," she said as she took a closer look at everyone's wings.

"We've all been struck by some mysterious illness. This is terrible."

"Fix them!" one of the cheerhexers demanded. "That's what you do, right? You make things look better."

"Oh, what a good idea. I can try." As Farrah took her little wand from her pocket, Faybelle cringed. While she wanted her cheerhexers fixed, she didn't want Farrah or the other auditioning fairy to recover. Could fairy godmother magic actually *fix* a dark spell? Farrah pointed her wand at one of the cheerhexers. A trail of music and sparkles shot out the wand's end, and for a moment, everyone held their breath, waiting to see what would happen.

The wings remained limp. Farrah's face fell. "I'm sorry. My fairy godmother magic doesn't seem to work in this situation."

Faybelle exhaled with relief. The audition was still hers. But the cheerhexing problem remained. How could she solve that?

"I wonder if it's some kind of virus," said Dexter Charming. He stepped into the aisle and pushed his glasses up his nose. "Viruses spread quickly. That would explain how so many of you got it at the same time."

"A virus?" Justine asked.

"It makes sense," Farrah said.

All this chitchat is a waste of time, Faybelle thought. "Hey, Justine. Do you hexpect me to stand here all day? Let's do this!"

Silence fell over the Charmitorium. Everyone turned and stared at Faybelle. She realized her mistake. She'd let her guard down. She'd forgotten to act as if she cared. Did they suspect?

"Hey, how come *your* wings are working?" one of the cheerhexers asked.

"Yeah, how come?"

Faybelle held back a gulp. She flicked her wings. "There is a perfectly adequate explanation." She took a few steps forward. "Dark fairies have superior immune systems. Centuries of dealing with dark magic have made us stronger than other fairies."

"That does makes sense," Dexter said with a nod.

This seemed to satisfy the cheerhexers. Besides, they'd never dare question their team captain and future queen. At least, not in public. Or to her face.

Farrah tucked away her wand. "I think we should go to the infirmary. Maybe there's some medicine we can take."

"I shall escort you, fairy damsels!" Daring cried. He leaped across the seats and bounded into the aisle. Then, with a bow, he said in his most dashing voice, "Follow me."

Farrah and the other fairies followed, along with Ashlynn, Briar, and Meeshell, who wanted to help in whatever way they could.

Finally! Good riddance! Faybelle cleared her throat. "Are you ready?"

Justine took her seat. "Yes, I guess we'd better get back to business. Go ahead."

Faybelle delivered the monologue, the same one Farrah would have delivered if she hadn't been sabotaged. She took her time walking around the stage,

allowing everyone to admire her costume. Then she stood in the center, hands on hips, and, for maximum visual impact, she unfurled her wings in slow motion. They stood magnificent, catching the spotlights, casting rainbows upon the walls. And then she flew around the stage, delivering her lines, condemning the king and queen for not sending an invitation. As the monologue concluded, she cursed the princess to prick her finger and sleep for a hundred years.

There was nary a doubt in Faybelle's mind. The part was hers! Confidence coursed through her.

She took a long bow. Since her cheerhexers had left, there was no fervent applause. A few members of the audience seemed to appreciate her performance, but most looked wary, unsure of how to react. Did they suspect her of foul play? Or did they think her performance was foul? Or was that fear she saw in their eyes?

"When does practice begin?" she asked Justine. "I'm busy most afternoons with the Cheerhexing Squad, but I can squeeze in time after dinner."

Justine held up her clipboard and pointed to another name. "You don't have the part yet. There's still one more person trying out."

Faybelle snorted. "She left. With the other fairies. Remember?"

"No, I didn't," a voice called. "I'm still here."

Because the spotlight was blinding her, Faybelle couldn't see who was speaking. She shielded her eyes with her hand and stepped to the edge of the stage. "You have to be a fairy to try out for the wicked fairy queen," she said, her eyes scanning the faces.

"She doesn't have to be a fairy," Justine corrected. "She simply has to have wings and be able to fly."

Not a fairy? What treachery was this? Who else had wings? Who else could fly? This was impossible.

Then Faybelle's gaze stopped cold on a smiling face.

C.A. Cupid.

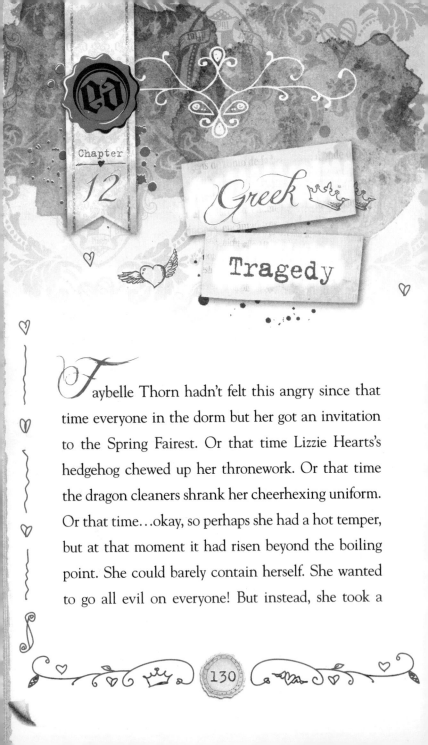

Greek

Tragedy

aybelle Thorn hadn't felt this angry since that time everyone in the dorm but her got an invitation to the Spring Fairest. Or that time Lizzie Hearts's hedgehog chewed up her thronework. Or that time the dragon cleaners shrank her cheerhexing uniform. Or that time…okay, so perhaps she had a hot temper, but at that moment it had risen beyond the boiling point. She could barely contain herself. She wanted to go all evil on everyone! But instead, she took a seat in the very back row, where no one could see her clenched jaw or blazing eyes.

C.A. Cupid stood on the stage, delivering some boring monologue. *Curses!* The wilted-wing spell only worked on fairies, not on whatever Cupid was. What was she, exactly? An adopted daughter of a Greek demigod? Whatever after. And what was up with all the pink? Pink hair, pink lip gloss, pink dress, pink shoes. And a big pink heart on top of her head. So much cuteness was nauseating. But aside from Cupid's questionable color obsession, the point was, she wasn't a fairy. Why would Justine allow a nonfairy to try out for such an important role? And to make the situation even more insulting, Cupid was the opposite of a villain. Her father was the god of love. Her destiny was to spread love to people. That was why she was always trying to matchmake everyone on campus. She had a MirrorCast show the cheerhexers were always watching called *Love Advice*. Cupid's *brilliant* advice was that people should follow their hearts. "Well, I've got news for you," Faybelle whispered. "I *am* following my heart, and my heart wants this part!"

If Faybelle hadn't been seething with rage, she might have noticed that Cupid wasn't much of an actor. Her delivery was okay, just not great. But though her wings were smaller than Faybelle's and solid, rather than translucent, she could fly. Justine seemed very pleased.

"Thanks so much," Justine said, taking the stage once again. She wrote something on her clipboard. "Let's take a break, everyone. Then we'll audition the rest of the parts."

"Wait," Faybelle said, scooting to the edge of her seat. "Who gets to play the wicked fairy queen?"

"I'll post the callback list tomorrow," Justine told her.

"But only two of us auditioned. Why do we have to audition again? That doesn't make sense. You should decide now. Me or Cupid."

"Well..." Justine hesitated. "I'd like to wait and

see what the doctor says. If Farrah is going to get better, then I'd like to give her the chance to try out. I think that's fair, don't you?"

"Yes," Cupid said, smiling at Justine. "I think that's super fair."

Faybelle blinked. "Fair?" Her fingers twitched, eager to deliver a bolt of magic. "Oh yes, we must be fair."

She glared at Cupid. If looks could kill, there would have been an explosion of pink on the stage. That little demigoddess had ruined everything! What a waste. All that time in the Vault of Lost Tales, searching through those crumbling books, inhaling dust. She was still picking cobwebs off her uniform. All that trouble and she had to compete against a nonfairy.

It was too much to bear. She was so filled with emotion that she felt she might burst. She needed to release some magic, she realized. Releasing just a little bit of magic would make her feel better.

She looked around the Charmitorium to make sure no one was watching, and then she pointed her

finger. She'd sear a hole in the seat in front of her. Just a little dust. Just a little *poof*. No one would get hurt.

But someone did get hurt. What Faybelle didn't realize was that when she'd cheerhexed the wilted-wing spell, she'd created magic so powerful that remnants had been left behind—a small dusting that still lingered on her finger. So when she released a jolt of fairy dust, it didn't sear a hole in the seatback. Instead, the magic ricocheted off the seatback and hit her in the chest. *Wham!*

"Huh?" Her back suddenly felt heavy, as if she were strapped to a book-filled backpack. "What the hex?"

As it dawned on her what might have happened, she slowly got to her feet. "No way," she said. "I did not just..." She unfurled her wings.

But the wings that she loved, the wings that she carefully tended and groomed, would not obey her command.

aybelle almost burst into tears. But she didn't. She maintained her cool demeanor. While Justine and the other students headed to the vending machines for their break, Faybelle walked down the row, up the aisle, and into the lobby. She'd pretend nothing had happened. No one would know that her wings didn't work. No one would see her in this weakened state. Never!

If word of this got around, she'd be forever after humiliated. To allow a spell to backfire would elicit comparisons to Raven Queen. That was an insult she couldn't bear.

And if Justine found out that Faybelle couldn't fly, she'd give the role of the wicked fairy queen to Cupid. A demigoddess playing a fairy queen? Not on Faybelle's watch!

As she stepped out of the building, the afternoon air felt different. It was a pleasant temperature, as usual, and tinged with the scent of warm cobblestones and buttercups. But the air did not embrace her as it usually did. It did not call to her, welcome her, or lift her. Without the buoyancy of her wings, she might as well have been wearing boulders on her feet. She was grounded, like a tree, like a mountain. How could the wingless stand this lack of freedom?

"Ms. Thorn!" The bellowing voice was unmistakable and could not be ignored.

"What now?" Faybelle grumbled to herself. She wanted to find someplace private. Someplace to gather her thoughts and process this situation. But the school's headmaster was walking straight for her.

Headmaster Grimm was very tall, which was why he often looked down his nose at his students. He had quite a lot of hair for a man of his advanced years, and his thick mustache was streaked with white. He bore a gentlemanly look, reminiscent of bygone days when men were dapper and ladies, elegant. The heavy key ring hanging from his belt symbolized his authority, for only he possessed the keys for many secret and forbidden rooms.

"Hello, Headmaster," Faybelle said. She folded her arms behind her back, hoping to hide the droopy wings. "You called?" She kept her voice calm, her gaze confident. But her mind reeled. Had she been found out? What would the punishment be? Dungeon detention, surely. Every good villain expected to be sent to dungeon detention on a regular basis, but if the headmaster tried to impose another kind of punishment, should she defend her actions? Her excuse was straightforward—a villain was supposed to act like a villain. A villain was supposed to pursue her destiny. And the headmaster was a firm believer in respecting one's destiny. He'd installed signs all over campus to remind students of this fact.

WE ARE THE CHILDREN OF DESTINY.

No, she couldn't confess. She'd have to play dumb. She could never admit that she'd become a victim of her own dark magic.

The headmaster halted. Then he looked up and waved. "Ms. Cupid, I require your presence as well!"

Faybelle cringed as Cupid landed next to her. "Hello, Headmaster Grimm," she said. "Do you need some love advice?"

"While I am a fan of your MirrorCast show, I am much too busy for matters of the heart." He smoothed his vest. "Ms. Thorn and Ms. Cupid, I just got off the MirrorPhone with Madam Baba Yaga. She would like both of you to report to the infirmary."

"I can't go," Faybelle explained. "I have a meeting of the Villain Club."

"While I appreciate your dedication to your

hextracurricular activities, Ms. Thorn, this is not open for debate." He raised his bushy eyebrows. "A mysterious wing ailment has spread among some students, and you must both be checked out. Do not delay. This appears to be very serious."

"Serious? Oh, that's terrible news," Cupid said. "I'll go right now."

"I don't need to go," Faybelle insisted.

"And why is that, Ms. Thorn? Do you believe you are impervious to disease?"

"Have you ever seen a dark fairy get sick?" she asked.

Cupid shifted her little golden bow onto her other shoulder. "I get sick sometimes. Last year during holiday I caught Athenian Acne. It lasted for a whole week. And one time I came down with the Herculean Flu. All the ambrosia in the world couldn't make me feel better."

Faybelle's wings might have twitched with annoyance, except they were currently as lifeless as woolen drapes. "May I be excused from this super-interesting

conversation? I have so many things to do." Did she dare call her mother and ask for help? Surely the Dark Fairy would know how to undo magic. But Faybelle had wanted to pull off this scheme on her own. To make her mother proud with her success, not disappoint her with failure.

"You may not be excused," Headmaster Grimm said. "This is a strange ailment that we have never before encountered. Therefore, it is of the utmost importance that all winged students undergo an examination. That is why I am *instructing* you to go to the infirmary." He did not use the word *ordering*, but that was his meaning. As the headmaster, he was the final decision-maker.

With a swift turn on his heels, he strode toward his office.

Faybelle groaned. "This is all your fault," she grumbled at Cupid. She started across the quad, fists clenched, teeth grinding. If Cupid hadn't signed up to audition, Faybelle wouldn't have been forced to add the cheer

factor to her spell and she'd be with her team, celebrating her victory at this very moment. *Stupid Cupid*.

An invasion of pink appeared out the corner of her eye. C.A. Cupid was walking beside her.

"What are you? My shadow?"

"We're going to the same place, so I thought it would be nice to walk together," Cupid said sweetly. "You seem upset."

"Your powers of observation are astounding."

"You're worried about your friends, aren't you? You and your teammates are very close."

"Yeah, that's it. I'm worried about my friends." Faybelle wanted to zap her with a dizzy spell and send her spinning to the ground. But there were too many witnesses milling about. How could she get rid of this pink problem?

Cupid ducked behind Faybelle, then reappeared. "Is there something wrong with your wings?"

"No."

"Really? They look kinda—"

"Kinda what?" Faybelle stopped walking and pointed a finger at Cupid. "Kinda what?"

Cupid shrugged. "Different."

"I'm tired. That's all. I stayed up late memorizing my monologue." Faybelle needed to deflect the conversation away from her wings. "What makes you think you can play the role of the wicked fairy queen better than I can play it?" she demanded.

"Oh, I'd *never* think that," Cupid said, her cheeks turning as pink as her dress. "Never. You were amazing. But Justine said she needed an actor who could fly, so I thought I should try out. I really don't care what part I get."

"If you don't care, then drop out."

"I don't want to drop out. I do want to be in the play. If Justine casts me as the wicked fairy queen, then I'll be happy to play that part. But if I get a part in the chorus, that will be fine, too." She ran her hand along her bow. "Theater is a huge tradition back home. Except all the plays are kind of depressing. All that Greek tragedy. I prefer love stories."

"Of course you do." The day was beginning to feel like a Greek tragedy. Everything was going wrong. Faybelle was supposed to be the hero of her own story, but this hero was not getting what she wanted.

"What kind of stories do you like?" Cupid asked.

The kind that ends with me in charge. "I don't have time for stories." Why was it taking so long to get to the infirmary? Walking was the slowest, most tedious means of travel ever invented.

Cupid kept jabbering. "I think you might be one of the busiest students on campus. I've watched you hurrying between practice and meetings. But you never seem super happy. Is there something missing in your life?"

"In case you hadn't noticed, Cupid, I'm not a guest on your MirrorCast show, so quit trying to analyze me. And in case you just woke up from a sleeping spell, I'm a villain. Villains aren't supposed to be *super* happy. We fester, we dwell, we're prone to years of melancholy. You know, proper villain emotions."

"But villains still feel love, right?"

Faybelle stopped walking again. They'd reached the stone steps that led to the infirmary. "What are you getting at?"

"Well…" Cupid raised her eyebrows. "Do you have love in your life?"

"I don't have time for love." Faybelle snorted. "Love makes you crazy. It makes you weak." Her gaze darted to the top step, where Ashlynn and Hunter were sitting. His arm was wrapped around her shoulders. They were whispering. "Love distracts you from the important stuff."

"I think love *is* important stuff," Cupid said. But Faybelle didn't care about Cupid's opinion. She marched up the steps, and as she did, Ashlynn and Hunter stood.

"Professor Yaga's in there, examining the fairies," Ashlynn told her. "She doesn't know what's wrong with them. She said she doesn't have a cure!"

"What are we going to do about regionals?" Hunter asked. "Do you think we'll have to forfeit?"

"No," Faybelle said firmly. "Champions *never* forfeit."

And while she believed that with every cell in her body, she had no idea how she was going to fix the mess she'd made. She reached out and grabbed Hunter's cloak, which was lying on the steps. "I need to borrow this."

With Cupid at her heels, she entered the infirmary.

Boiling

Blood

ven though it was plenty warm inside the stone building, Faybelle flung Hunter's cloak over her shoulders and attached it at her neck. It hung all the way to her shins—more than enough fabric to cover her wilted wings.

The infirmary was an old-fashioned name for the student clinic. Small nurse fairies tended the facility's patients, applying bandages, dispensing medicine, mending broken bones, that sort of stuff. Farrah, the two first-year fairies, and the six cheerhexers were

sitting on benches in the waiting room. The cheer-hexers didn't cheer Faybelle's entrance as they usually did. They all sat listless, shoulders drooping, expressions heavy with worry. No twinkle in their eyes. No sparkle in their presence. They were the saddest bunch of fairies Faybelle had ever seen.

"Hi, Faybelle. Hi, Cupid," Farrah said. "What are you doing here?"

"Headmaster Grimm sent us," Cupid explained. "We're supposed to get our wings examined."

The blue in Farrah's eyes had dulled. They looked gray. "Oh, I hope you're not sick," she said.

"Of course I'm not sick," Faybelle insisted.

"We're waiting for our results," Farrah explained. She held a cotton ball to her index finger. "They took a drop of blood for a blood test."

Madam Baba Yaga stood at the end of the hall. Slightly hunched over, she beckoned with a gnarled finger. "Ms. Thorn, Ms. Cupid, this way, please."

The girls joined the professor in an examination room. A nurse fairy stuck a thermometer in Cupid's mouth while another wrapped a blood pressure cuff around her arm.

"We must take your vital signs," Madam Baba Yaga explained. "Take a seat, Ms. Thorn, and wait your turn."

"This is a waste of everyone's time because I'm not sick," Faybelle insisted.

As Madam Baba Yaga supervised, a nurse fairy pricked Cupid's finger and placed a drop of blood into a little vial. Madam Baba Yaga held the vial up to her nose. She sniffed it. She added a pinch of green powder, then murmured some magical words. The blood did not respond.

"Didn't you hear me?" Faybelle said huffily. "I'm not sick."

"That remains to be seen." Madam Baba Yaga inspected Cupid's wings with a magnifying glass. "Are they working as usual?" she asked.

"Oh yes," Cupid said. "I would have flown here, but Faybelle was walking, so I walked with her. My wings are perfect." To demonstrate, she lifted herself off the floor and fluttered around the room.

"Indeed." Madam Baba Yaga wrote some notes in a file. "You may be excused, Ms. Cupid. It would appear that you are not affected."

"Okay. Thanks." Cupid hurried toward the door but then turned. "Good luck, Faybelle."

Faybelle paced like a caged beast. She began to sweat beneath the cloak.

"You appear to be a bit agitated," Madam Baba Yaga observed.

"I'm not agitated!" Faybelle bellowed.

Madam Baba Yaga stared at the cloak. Then she waved her hand at the nurse fairies. "Leave us," she told them. They flitted from the room. The door closed, and Faybelle and the professor were alone. A bead of sweat rolled down Faybelle's nose.

"Wouldn't you be more comfortable without that heavy cloak?" the professor asked.

"No. It's the latest style. I love it."

"Really?"

"Yes, really. In fact, I'm going to call the tailor at Fairy Fashion and Finery and order a dozen more."

She wiped the sweat with the back of her hand. "I'll go do that right now." She started toward the door, but Madam Baba Yaga blocked her path.

"Ms. Thorn, I do not have to *inspect* your wings to know that they have been wilted." She pulled a twig from her matted hair and, using its blunt end, she scratched the back of her neck. "My eyes may be old and bloodshot, but I can clearly see that you've lost your sparkle."

Was this true? Faybelle looked in a mirror that hung above the examination room's sink. She did look different. Her skin was less luminous. Her eyes were dull. She looked…Oh horror of horrors! Could it be true? She looked *ordinary*.

Madam Baba Yaga tossed the twig aside, then picked up another file. Faybelle's name was written on the file's cover. "You have no record of illness," she said, "aside from a few bumps and bruises from cheerhexing. Yet here you are, along with nine other fairies, stricken by a mysterious ailment. Is there something you'd like to tell me?"

Faybelle turned away from the mirror. "Like what?" She wasn't lying, just playing dumb.

Madam Baba Yaga plucked the vial from the counter. Cupid's drop of blood wobbled from the movement. "When coming into contact with the magic detection powder, Ms. Cupid's blood remained unaltered. However…" She picked up a different vial. It also contained a drop of blood. She sprinkled green powder into the vial. The drop began to boil. A puff of black steam shot out the top. "This blood shows clear signs that it has recently been exposed to dark magic. This blood belongs to Ms. Goodfairy."

"Really?" Faybelle examined her nails. "How dreadfully uninteresting." Another bead of sweat trailed down her neck. If the professor wanted a confession, she'd have to try much harder.

"Do you remember my advice on cheerhexing? I clearly told you not to use your magic touch unwisely. I advised you to hone your skills slowly. Broken teacups are one thing, but attacking your fellow fairies—"

"I didn't *attack* them," Faybelle blurted.

They stood in silence for a moment. The cloak was smothering. Faybelle needed fresh air. She backed up until her legs came into contact with the edge of a chair. Then she sat. She wanted to crumple into a ball. Her wings felt so heavy. Her heart felt heavy, too.

When Madam Baba Yaga spoke, her voice was gentle. "The spell will wear off?"

"Yes," Faybelle admitted. "In a moon's span."

"Good." The professor washed the vials in the sink. "I'm curious, Ms. Thorn. What was your motive for attacking fellow students?"

"To eliminate my competition."

"I see." She nodded, but she didn't look like she approved. "You will refrain from magic until this situation is resolved."

"No magic?" Faybelle gasped.

"Do not press your luck, Ms. Thorn."

Faybelle went silent.

"No magic. None at all. Do you understand?"

Faybelle groaned. "Yes." The punishment could have been much worse. She could have been expelled, but, still, no magic felt harsh.

Madam Baba Yaga opened the examination room door. "There are times in life, Ms. Thorn, when magic is not necessary. When the terms of competition should be fair and square."

"A villain doesn't fight *fair and square*," Faybelle said. "A villain does what she has to do to win."

Madam Baba Yaga pressed her fingertips together and gave Faybelle a knowing look. "Sometimes it is the victory won fairly that proves to be the most rewarding. But, alas, here you are. No role in the play. No regionals. No flight."

"Whatever after," Faybelle grumbled as she wrapped the cloak around her shoulders and trudged away. She'd deal with this in her own way. Her own *wicked* way.

Dark Fairy

Discussion

*M*adam Baba Yaga told the fairies that their wings would recover in a moon's span.

"Four weeks?" the cheerhexers cried.

"What about regionals?"

"We can't compete with regular cheers."

"How embarrassing."

"We're famous for our flying formations."

"What are we going to do?" They looked beseechingly at their leader.

Faybelle put her hands on her hips. "Who am I?" she asked them.

"Faybelle Thorn, daughter of the Dark Fairy."

"That's correct. So stop all your whining and have some confidence. I will figure this out, and we will claim that trophy!"

Because the wilted-wing sickness wasn't contagious, the fairies were allowed to leave the infirmary and were told to go about life as usual. But that was impossible, for there was nothing usual about being earthbound. The sky was calling. But the fairies could not answer.

The situation was the hot topic on Blondie's Mirror-Cast show that evening. It hadn't taken long for Blondie to get the scoop. Being in the know about everything, she reported that Faybelle had been infected. Had Cupid told her? Possibly, but Blondie never revealed her secret sources. Or was it simply that Faybelle couldn't hide the truth? It was obvious she had no flight. And covering her wings with Hunter's cloak only drew attention to the matter—like a bald

guy trying to cover his scalp with an ill-fitting toupee. But even though everyone knew, Faybelle couldn't bear to have them stare at her wings, so she tossed Hunter's cloak aside and chose a shimmering cape she'd worn to a masquerade ball last year. At least it didn't make her sweat.

"What does this mean for your original play, *Once Upon a Spell?*" Blondie asked Justine during her show.

"Well, callbacks are tomorrow afternoon," Justine said. "If neither Faybelle nor Farrah gets better, it looks like the part of the wicked fairy queen will be going to Cupid. I just hope Cupid doesn't get sick. I really need a flying actor."

Blondie looked into the camera. "Did you hear that, Cupid? Take your vitamins and get plenty of sleep. You can't get sick or Justine's play will be an epic fairy fail."

Faybelle turned off her MirrorPad. Too bad there wasn't some sort of fairytale flu spreading across campus. And too bad she'd been forbidden to use magic. She could steal Cupid's voice but make it look like laryngitis. She could shoot pixie music into her ear and make it seem like an earache. But even if she could use magic, it would be foolish to attack Cupid. Madam Baba Yaga would figure it out. She'd punish Faybelle. Everyone would know. And Faybelle would never get the role.

Oh, to be wingless *and* magicless was torture! How did ordinary students stand it?

Somehow, some way, she would keep Cupid from going to callbacks. Better yet, she'd persuade Cupid to drop out of the play entirely. Then Justine would be forced to wait for the wilted-wing spell to wear off. What other choice would she have? But that also brought risk, because the spell would wear off for *all* the fairies, meaning Farrah would be in the running again. Faybelle versus Farrah? She would be back where she'd started. What a mess!

She leaned against her closet door.

"You okay?" Bunny asked. She sat at her desk, working on thronework.

Faybelle was as far from being okay as an ogre was from being charming. Her shoulders were aching, her neck sore. Her wings had always felt weightless, as if spun from air, but now it was like carrying a backpack filled with stones. "I'm fine," she lied, though the bottoms of her feet throbbed something fierce. *Show no weakness.*

"You sure?" Bunny pushed her top hat away from her eyes. Her long ears twitched. "You don't look fine. I mean, you've got dark circles under your eyes. And you're not complaining about my carrot tops, like you usually do."

It was true. Faybelle's energy level was at a low simmer, at best.

Her MirrorPhone rang. Her mother's face appeared on the screen. "Darling, I just heard. Madam Baba Yaga assures me that you will be fine. Your wings will recover completely. I'll send the driver immediately to pick you up."

Faybelle stepped into the hallway so she could speak to her mother in private. "Mom, I can't go home. I can't miss classes or I'll fall behind. I have too

much work to do. I have Villain Club, cheerhexers to lead. I'm swamped."

"Nonsense. Your health is more important than schoolwork. I'll call Headmaster Grimm and demand that you be given special permission to leave. You must recover here, my darling. Healing from dark magic requires special care."

"Did Professor Yaga tell you this was dark magic?" Faybelle asked.

"I know when dark magic is afoot," she replied. "No one needs to inform me of such matters. I *am* dark magic, as are you, my love."

"Yes, but you've never been hit by a dark magic spell." Faybelle cringed, pained by deep feelings of shame. "You never..." She couldn't say it. Couldn't speak the horrid truth. Faybelle looked away. How could she admit that she'd made such an amateur mistake? That she was a victim of her own magic? That she'd paralyzed her own wings?

The Dark Fairy's voice boomed from the speaker.

"I will demand an inquiry. Someone attacked my child. This will not stand!"

"No, Mom, don't." Faybelle looked around to make certain no one was eavesdropping. The only movement was Lizzie Hearts's plump hedgehog waddling between rooms, searching for treats. "I don't want you to make a big deal about this. I don't want you to investigate. I'm old enough to fight my own battles." *And I'm old enough to clean up my own messes.*

Her mother looked at her. Though the Dark Fairy was far away and her face was on a small screen, Faybelle felt the power of her mother's gaze. "Faybelle, did you...?" Her mother paused. Did she suspect the truth? "Very well," she said. "Fight your battle. But if, at any time, I sense you need me, I will fly at lightning speed to fight by your side." She blew a kiss.

"Thanks, Mom." Did other villains have such good relationships with their parents? That might make for an interesting topic of discussion at the next Villain Club meeting.

Back in the room, Spindle yapped at Faybelle's feet. She picked him up and nuzzled his cheek. He chewed on her finger, his tail wagging as if charged by its own motor. "I'm going to dinner," she told him. "I'll bring you back a treat."

"I can't go," Bunny said, hunched over a hext-book. "Could you bring me a salad?"

"What do you think?"

"I'm guessing...no." Bunny's ears drooped.

"I've taught you well." Then she whispered in Spindle's furry ear, "But for you, my love, I'll bring back whatever your little heart desires." Now, if only she could get what her heart desired.

Chapter 16

A Golden Opportunity

$\mathcal{S}$unday morning came. Faybelle had barely slept a wink. The combination of worry and discomfort had taken its toll.

Dressed and headed for breakfast, she walked down staircase after staircase, trying to focus her thoughts. She still wanted to play the wicked fairy queen. She'd put so much time and effort into getting the role, and quitting was never an option. So it seemed the next thing to do was to remove Cupid from the competition. But Faybelle would have to

manage this without her cheer factor. Without any sort of fairy magic. How could she do that?

As she entered the Castleteria, students turned to stare, but their eyes were not filled with fear or respect. It was a softer, concerned look. Pity. They felt sorry for her. On a normal day, she would have whacked them with her wings as she flew past. "What are you looking at?" she snapped at Gus Crumb, son of Gretel.

"I vas not looking at anything," Gus said, his mouth half stuffed with pie. "I vas looking at nothing."

"I am not *nothing*," she corrected. "I am still the daughter of the Dark Fairy. Do not forget that." She raised her voice so that it spread to every pair of ears in the Castleteria. "This is a momentary inconvenience. My superior flying skills will return. But be forewarned—if you anger me now, you will feel my wrath later!" A pair of cleaning fairies bowed their heads respectfully. But Apple White leaped from her bench and hurried to Faybelle's side.

"Oh, you're so good at the whole villain thing," she said, smiling so hard that two perfect dimples appeared

on her round cheeks. "I wish *my* villain would take her role more seriously. Anyhoo, here's a little something for you. Charm you later." And off she went.

She'd handed Faybelle a card. Faybelle opened it.

A little birdie told me you were sick.
Get well soon.
        Apple White

It was cringeworthy, but also kind of nice.

Faybelle joined her six cheerhexers at their usual table. Seeing their wings hanging lifeless against their backs was a shocking sight indeed, but they looked different in other ways. They were dressed in drab sweatpants and sweatshirts. No one had bothered to comb hair or gloss lips. And they weren't

bickering as usual. They were sitting quietly, barely touching their food. When they saw her coming, they cheered, in very quiet voices, "Faybelle, Faybelle, she's the one....She's the one...and...something, something," then sighed. They didn't even have the energy to finish the sentence. Or to rhyme.

"Why aren't you wearing your uniforms?" Faybelle asked as she sat.

"What's the point?"

"Why bother?"

"I'm so depressed."

"Me too."

Faybelle glanced around the table. "Where's my food?" she asked. Her team always got her food and drink, but there was no tray waiting for her.

"We forgot."

"Well, I'm here and I'm hungry, so go get me something," Faybelle said.

"You want us to *walk* all the way over there?" The food counter was only a few yards away.

"Walking's soooo hard."

"I hate walking."

"I tried skipping, and that's even worse."

"I can't even cartwheel. My wings throw off my balance."

"Why did this happen?"

The six looked to Faybelle for an answer. Their leader, their future queen. Faybelle grabbed one of their glasses and took a long drink. They were still looking at her, waiting for wisdom. They needed a pep talk. "Listen up," she said. "We're going to get better. We're going to fly again and do cartwheels and win cheerhexing championships. You can bet on that. But right now we've got a bigger problem. I need you to hocus focus." She motioned them in for a huddle. "I don't want Cupid to get that part. Understand? If I can't play the wicked fairy queen, no one can. So I need Cupid to quit. But it can't look like I *made* her quit. Got it?"

"No."

"Not really."

"Are you going to drink *all* of my juice?"

Faybelle snapped her fingers. "Pay attention. How can we get Cupid to quit the play?"

"Oh, I know. You could turn her into a toad."

"Or push her into the wishing well so she ends up in Wonderland."

"Or cast a hiccup spell so she can't say her lines."

"No, no, no." Faybelle groaned with frustration. "I can't do any of those things. I can't cast dark magic or they'll know it was me. It needs to look like Cupid made this decision herself." A few of the students at the next table had turned and were staring over their shoulders. Faybelle drew her team closer and lowered her voice. "We can't talk details here. I'll meet you on the field in fifteen. And I'll expect some sort of brilliant and devious plan. Go."

"Walk to the field?"

"That's such a long way."

"We could call a carriage. I have an app."

"Oh, good idea."

As the cheerhexers dragged themselves from the Castleteria, Faybelle reluctantly got her own breakfast. She helped herself to scrambled goose eggs, country purple potatoes, and a crisp red apple. But she'd only eaten a few bites when a fluttering sound drew her attention. C.A. Cupid landed, tray in hand. "Hi, Faybelle, mind if I join you?"

"Yes."

"Yes, you mind? Or yes, I can join you?"

Faybelle skewered a potato. "What do *you* think?"

"Oh great. Thanks." Cupid chose the bench across from Faybelle. She placed her tray on the table, then sat. Apparently the little Greek demi-goddess was an expert on love but not sarcasm.

She was as pink as always. Even her eyelids had a generous swish of sparkly pink shadow. She'd chosen a Greek yogurt with honey for breakfast. "So I've been thinking about something."

Not only was she invading Faybelle's personal space, but she also required conversation. "If you don't mind, I'm trying to eat," Faybelle told her.

"Me too." Cupid took a bite of yogurt. "But the

something I've been thinking about is you. I think I've figured it out."

Did she suspect the truth? Did she know Faybelle had cast the wilted-wing spell? Faybelle set her fork aside. "Do go on. I'm tingling with hexpectation."

"You said that dark fairies never get sick, yet here you are, just like the others, with the same illness. But did you know that our immune systems are influenced by our emotions? Sadness, depression, and stress make us more vulnerable to disease. But joy, laughter, and love make us stronger."

More feel-good mumbo jumbo. "I've heard enough," Faybelle said. "You can leave now."

"But I haven't told you my idea."

"So not interested."

Cupid wasn't discouraged by Faybelle's snarky tone. "I think the reason you got sick is because you need more love in your life. If you want, I could help make a match for you."

"Matchmake? Don't you dare shoot me with one

of those arrows." She pointed to the golden quiver that hung from Cupid's shoulder.

"Oh, I'd never do that. I only use my arrows in emergency situations because they are so powerful. Did you know that one of my arrows would make you so loopy you wouldn't be able to think clearly? You'd quit your clubs, stop going to class. You wouldn't want to do anything but pursue love." She giggled. "Anyway, I believe you should start with a date, meet at Hocus Latte—that's a good place to talk. Or do an activity, like go for a…"

"What did you say?" Faybelle interrupted.

"I said do an activity, go for a—"

"No, you said something about quitting clubs." Suddenly this conversation was taking an interesting turn.

"Oh right. Well, my arrows are very powerful." Cupid set her quiver and bow onto the table. "They contain an ancient Greek god love potion. It changes the chemistry of your brain so all you can think about is love. It *literally* makes you lovesick. You don't want to do any of your normal activities."

"Really?"

"I have to be very cautious about using my arrows. You should hear my dad's stories. He caused so much trouble. That's why I like to matchmake the old-fashioned way."

Faybelle reached out and touched the golden quiver. "What happens, exactly? Does the effect take place immediately?"

"Oh yes, instantly."

"And how long does it last?"

"It can last for a whole week. But then it starts to wear off. If that person was meant to fall in love, they will stay in love. But if it wasn't meant to be, they will have no lingering effects."

Greek god magic wasn't fairy magic. Which meant that Faybelle wouldn't be casting a spell. Could the perfect plan have fallen right into her lap?

"How can you shoot someone with an arrow and not hurt them?"

"These aren't regular arrows." Cupid took one out and showed it to Faybelle. It was small and golden.

"My arrows dissolve the instant they hit someone. You can't even feel it pierce the skin. I have the worst aim ever after. What if I miss and hit the wrong person? I can't count the number of times I've almost shot myself in the foot." She laughed. Then she slid the arrow back into the quiver. "Shooting myself with my own magic. Can you believe that?"

Faybelle glowered at her. "You'd have to be totally lame to hit yourself with your own magic."

"Hey, Cupid," a voice called. Ashlynn and Briar were standing a few yards away. "You want to come with us?" Ashlynn asked. "We're taking breakfast to Farrah. She's feeling super sad about her wings."

Briar held up a platter. "We thought we'd cheer her up with some fairyberry pancakes." The whipped cream jiggled.

"Oh, I want to help cheer her up, too," Cupid called. "Bye," she said to Faybelle, and she flew after the princesses.

Faybelle smiled. Her hands closed around the bow and the quiver, which Cupid had left behind.

Twinkle Toes

hen Faybelle arrived at the athletic field, she was surprised to find that the six cheerhexers were not there as instructed. Apparently, the chariot app hadn't worked, so they'd only walked halfway before deciding they were too tired to take another step. So Faybelle had to go look for them. She found them draped across benches next to the swan pool. The sun was shining and the fairies weren't paying any attention to their limp wings.

Faybelle pulled a travel-sized spray bottle of sunscreen from her pocket. "Your wing tips are going to burn," she scolded. She walked around and spritzed each fairy. How could they be so negligent? This wilted-wing spell was clearly taking a bigger toll than Faybelle had realized. It was wilting more than just the fairies' wings. "Did you come up with a plan?" she asked, returning the sunblock to her pocket.

"We're too tired to think."

"Our feet are killing us."

"We need jet packs or something."

"Yeah, jet packs."

Faybelle had never been a fan of complaining. Actions always spoke louder than words. "Hello?" she said. "In case you hadn't noticed, I'm in the exact same condition, and you don't hear me whining." *Or confessing that I'm the cause of all this*, she silently added.

She snapped her fingers, trying to get their full attention. "Listen up. I will overlook your total disregard of my instructions *this one time* because I have already devised a plan, and it's both brilliant and devious." She opened her shimmering cape to reveal the quiver and bow, which she'd slung over her shoulder. Faybelle looked around to make sure no one was within earshot. The only creatures nearby were the swans, and Duchess Swan, who could turn into a swan, was not among them. It appeared the coast was clear. "These are Cupid's arrows," Faybelle explained. Still, the fairies said nothing. "Don't you get it? I'm going to aim one at her foot."

"Why?"

"Are you taking archery or something?"

"Are you mad at her foot?"

"No! I'm not mad at her foot." For fairies, these six were unbelievably daft sometimes. "If she gets struck by her arrow, she'll go lovesick crazy, and she won't care about being in the play. She'll only care about love. Get it? She won't go to callbacks this afternoon. She won't get the part."

"I still think it would be easier to turn her into a toad."

"It might be easier, but that kind of magic could be traced back to me." Faybelle closed her cape again.

"This plan is brilliant because this is Cupid's magic, not my magic. People will think she shot herself in the foot. It's foolproof. But I need your help."

They groaned with exasperation. How could she motivate them? "Cupid thinks she's better than us because she can fly and we can't." Faybelle waited for those words to sink in.

Despite their fatigue, little sparkles ignited in their eyes. "We don't like Cupid."

"No, we don't."

"She can fly and we can't."

"That makes us so mad."

"Let's get her."

"Yes, let's."

And then, with a sudden burst of energy, they cheered. "Faybelle, Faybelle, shish, boom, bah. Shoot Cupid in the foot, rah, rah, rah!"

There was nothing like an evil plan to bring the cheerhexers together once again.

It didn't take long to find Cupid. She'd already

posted signs all over campus about her lost bow and arrows.

LOST

A golden bow and quiver
of golden arrows.
If found, please return to me, Cupid.
I'll be down at the stables, feeding
Peggy, my Pegasus.

Getting to the stable required more walking, but they finally made it. The stable doors stood wide open. Faybelle told the cheerhexers to wait beneath a grand oak tree while she surveyed the situation. She crept to the barn and peeked around the doorframe. Cupid was standing in the middle of the barn, brushing a lovely white winged pony. The pony's ears pricked and she glanced at Faybelle, but Cupid didn't notice. Faybelle couldn't have wished for a better location. There was no one around to witness the devious deed except a pony who couldn't speak. *Hexcellent.*

Cupid, however, wasn't going to be as easy a target as Faybelle had hoped, because as the little demigoddess brushed, she kept moving. She flapped her wings so she could reach the back of the pony's neck. Then she moved to Peggy's rump to brush the tail. Next, she darted toward the front leg. She was flitting around like a pink bumblebee.

Faybelle hurried back to the cheerhexers, who were now lounging in the oak tree's shade. "Okay, she's in there, so here's what we'll do. I need you to go inside and persuade her to take off her shoes."

"How are we going to do that?"

"Yeah, how?"

Faybelle groaned. "Do I have to think of everything?"

"Yep."

"Uh-huh."

Wasn't *that* the truth! "Okay, so tell her that you love her shoes and you want to try them on. Or tell her that she stepped in Pegasus poop. Whatever! Just get her barefoot and then distract her so she doesn't see me. Got it?"

They nodded. And off they trudged in their sweat-pants. And because they weren't used to tiptoeing, they made as much noise as a herd of minotaurs.

Faybelle pulled an arrow from the quiver and held it against the bow. She'd never shot an arrow before, but how difficult could it be? She hurried back to the barn. A stack of hay bales provided the perfect hiding spot. She stepped behind it. The barn housed all sorts of hoofed creatures, so the odor was pungent.

"Hi, Cupid," the cheerhexers said, their heavy footsteps kicking up bits of straw. Peggy snorted.

Cupid stopped brushing and landed on the ground. Her little wings fluttered their welcome. "Hi. What are you all doing here?"

"We came to see you."

"Yep, to see you."

"Really?" Her wings relaxed. "Do you need love advice?"

"We want you to take off your shoes."

Faybelle rolled her eyes. At an upcoming Villain Club meeting, she'd need to have a discussion about *subtlety*.

"My shoes?" Cupid looked down at her feet. The shoes were pink, of course, decorated with little rhinestone hearts. "Do you like them?"

"Love them."

"Adore them."

"We don't like you because you can fly."

"But we think your shoes are spelltacular!"

"Really?" Cupid didn't seem to notice the insult amid all the compliments. "I special-ordered them from the Glass Slipper. Would you like to try them?" She slipped one off and handed it to the nearest fairy. Cupid's toes twinkled with pink polish. As she reached for the other shoe, Faybelle smirked with satisfaction. How easy was this?

Faybelle pulled back the bow and prepared to aim when the sound of approaching footsteps drew everyone's attention. Faybelle stepped into the hay bales' shadow as Humphrey Dumpty entered the barn. He stopped dead in his tracks when he spotted the cheerhexers. His round face turned crimson.

"Humphrey?" Cupid asked. "You okay?"

"Yes." He gulped, then adjusted his thick glasses. "I was looking for you, Cupid. I saw your sign taped to the tree outside the Castleteria."

"Did you find my bow and quiver?" she asked hopefully.

"No, but I wanted to ask you something. Something…personal." He fiddled with his suspenders, which held his pants way too high.

"Sure, this sounds important." She turned to the fairies. "Give me a moment and then we can talk about my shoes." With one foot bare, she led Humphrey over to the stack of hay bales, far enough from the fairies for a private conversation but close enough so Faybelle could hear every word. "What's up?"

"You know how I tried out for the forgetful prince?" His voice had a squeaky quality. "Well, it's the leading male role, and that means Daring Charming will get it, of course."

"Why do you think that?"

"Because he always gets the lead. Nobody sees me as a leading man. I'm the tech guy. I'm the nerd." Cupid didn't argue with him. "And if everyone sees me that way, then Justine won't be any different. So I was wondering, well, do you think you could help me get girls to take me more seriously? Maybe help me get a date?"

Try not tucking your sweater-vest into your pants, Faybelle thought as she peeked around a hay bale.

"The key, Humphrey, is to be yourself," Cupid said calmly. "The right girl will love you for who you are."

"Yeah, but if you help me get a date, then Justine might see me differently. She might give me the leading role. I know it's a long shot, but I'd like to try."

As Cupid listened to Humphrey, she stood perfectly still, her bare foot in view. Faybelle pulled

back the bow. *Ready…aim…* But just as her fingers released, Peggy, the Pegasus pony, lunged forward and knocked into the bales, throwing Faybelle off balance. The arrow soared through the air. Faybelle landed on the floor.

"Whoa, Peggy, what's wrong?" Cupid grabbed Peggy's reins. "Do you want some hay?"

Faybelle scrambled to her feet. Still hidden, she sneaked a look. Cupid's bare foot looked untouched. Cupid wasn't wearing a goofy, lovestruck grin. Faybelle had missed her target! Where had the arrow gone?

A moment later, that question was answered.

Humphrey 👑

the Hunk?

"Hi, Humphrey." One of the cheerhexers skipped forward and put a hand on Humphrey's arm. "My, my, don't you look handsome today." She batted her lashes.

"I do?" Humphrey's crown fell right off his head.

Oh my godmother! Faybelle couldn't believe it. The arrow had struck one of her cheerhexers. Faybelle's misfortune was at an all-time epic high. Luck had completely abandoned her. Sure, that particular cheerhexer had wilted wings *and* lovesickness, but

that couldn't compare with the humiliation Faybelle would feel if she lost the role to Cupid!

She grabbed another arrow and set it against the bow. *Stand still, Cupid!* she silently urged. *Ready…aim…*

Cupid moved. Again. What was the matter with her? She was as fidgety as a flea. The arrow soared past Cupid's leg and hit another cheerhexer. Right in the shin. As the arrow dissolved, a goofy grin spread across the cheerhexer's face. "Oh, Humphrey," she cooed. "Where have you been all my life?"

"Uh, I've mostly been in the Tech Club room. We've been recalibrating a pumpkin stagecoach motor."

Faybelle couldn't believe this was happening. Without even thinking, she grabbed another arrow, narrowed her eyes, and took aim. Cupid moved again. The arrow whizzed past Peggy's tail and hit a third cheerhexer. This one took her arrow in the shoulder.

"Oh, Humphrey," the latest victim gushed. "That sounds so hexciting. Can I recalibrate with you?"

Humphrey was speechless. Three fairies were hanging on to his arms, batting their lashes, and smiling at him. "You see?" Cupid said happily. "I told you, just be yourself."

Faybelle set down the bow and quiver and took a seat on a bale of hay. It was as if the universe was mocking her. Everything she'd tried to accomplish over the last few days had gone wrong. Would she have to join Raven in the Vault of Lost Tales, looking for a book to help them both with their backfiring spells? Would nothing go right?

The three lovestruck cheerhexers began bickering. "I saw him first."

"No, I did."

"He's mine."

Because they were so deliriously eager for Humphrey's attention, the other three, who hadn't been stuck by arrows, began to wonder why Humphrey had suddenly become such a hot commodity. Why hadn't they noticed this incredibly popular prince? Obviously, he was much more than he seemed. They

refused to be left out of this game. So they began to woo him, as well. "Hi, Humphrey."

"Don't forget about us."

"Humphrey, Humphrey, hear our cry, you're the cutest"—*clap*—"tech guy." They began to push, shove, and elbow, trying to get close to him.

"What's happening?" Humphrey asked with a look of sheer terror.

Then chaos erupted. One fairy aimed a spell at another. Horns popped up on that fairy's head.

"Hey!" She aimed back. "Take that." A tail sprouted.

"No, you take that!" A nose turned into a snout.

"I'd better put you in your stall, where you'll be safe," Cupid told Pegasus.

"I think I've changed my mind about dating," Humphrey said as fairy dust filled the air. He grabbed his crown and began backing toward the barn door. Faybelle might have been annoyed by the cheerhexers' bickering, but they were creating a masterful diversion.

"Hey, he's getting away!"

"Oh, Humphrey, my love, come back!"

Humphrey was on the move, running as fast as his skinny legs could carry him. The six cheerhexers, despite their complaints about sore feet, took up the chase.

Leaving Faybelle and Cupid alone in the barn. Finally.

Faybelle gripped the bow so tightly her fingers went numb. This was her last chance. She'd get it right this time. She stepped out from behind the hay bales. Cupid now stood in the barn's doorway, shielding her eyes and watching the cheerhexers pursue Humphrey up the lane.

"How strange," Cupid muttered to herself. She wasn't flitting about. Her pink toenail polish twinkled in the sunlight.

Faybelle took one step, then another. She moved stealthily, like a serpent sneaking up on its prey. She'd get close enough so there'd be no way to miss. Not this time! She took aim and—

Cupid whipped around. "Oh, you found them!" Her wings beat the air as she dove at Faybelle, grabbing the bow and quiver. "I'm so relieved to have them back. I

188

don't know what might have happened if they'd fallen into the wrong hands. Thank you so much." She hugged her precious bow and quiver to her chest.

Faybelle stood in shocked silence.

Cupid gave Faybelle a concerned look. "You know, that wilted-wing sickness is making your cheerhexers act very odd. You might want to take them to Professor Yaga again." She slipped her shoe back on. "I'd better go. I think Humphrey might need my help. Oh, and I also need to get ready for callbacks. Have a great day, and thanks again for finding my stuff." She gave Faybelle a happy wave and off she flew.

It was over. There was nothing left to do. Faybelle Thorn, daughter of the Dark Fairy, captain of the Cheerhexing Squad, president of the Villain Club, had failed. She'd hurt herself, and her cheerhexers. She'd lost.

A scream welled up from the depths of her being. She aimed her face toward the barn ceiling and let the scream loose. It erupted, the sound of anguish, waking the sleeping bats and disturbing a family of mice who'd been sitting on a rafter, eating corn kernels.

"What are you looking at?" she grumbled at Peggy, who was chewing on alfalfa. "Haven't you ever seen a loser before?"

Faybelle trudged up the lane. Maybe she would go home. Lie low. Wallow in self-pity. Lost in troubled thoughts, she didn't hear her MirrorPhone chime its reminder that cheerhexing practice was about to begin. She didn't even notice that she was walking straight past the field. "Hey, Faybelle!" Hunter ran up to her. "Where are you going? Aren't we going to work on the pyramid? Where's the rest of the team?"

Holly, Nina, and Farrah stood by his side, pompoms in hand, waiting for Faybelle's answer.

"They're not coming," Faybelle said. *I messed things up, big-time.*

Hunter scratched his head. "But I thought you wanted us to get the pyramid perfected for regionals."

"I do. But—" How could she explain? She took a deep breath. "The other fairies won't be joining us today. Or tomorrow. I don't know when they'll be back to normal. When *we'll* be back to normal." She glanced at Farrah. "We'll have to forfeit." Hunter, Holly, and Nina gasped. Then, with heavy shoulders and drooping wings, Faybelle continued walking.

"Faybelle, wait," Farrah called. She ran up to her, her uniform's skirt beating against her legs.

"Leave me alone," Faybelle snipped.

"But—"

"What are you doing here, anyway? I thought you were feeling *sad*."

"I am feeling sad," Farrah said, matching Faybelle's stride. "But I didn't want to let you down. I know how much this team means to you."

A lump rose in Faybelle's throat. Despite the fact that she was stuck with three wingless students, the Cheerhexing Squad meant *everything* to her. She was the captain. The leader. But she was also the reason they'd have to forfeit. She'd let them down.

"It doesn't have to be this way." Farrah darted in front of Faybelle, blocking her path. "You can fix this."

Faybelle stopped walking. She arched an eyebrow. "What do you mean?"

"When I fix things, I make them look better, or taste better. They *seem* better. And it's just a temporary fix until midnight. But you have bigger powers. You can truly fix things. You can make this right." Farrah smiled sweetly.

"What exactly are you insinuating?"

"Look, I know what you think about us Good-fairys. I know you think our magic is unimportant. But we are very observant. We know the difference between good magic and dark magic. And I know that my wings didn't wilt from some virus." Why didn't she sound angry? What was that tone to her voice? Was it *forgiveness*?

"You can clean up this mess," Farrah continued. "Remember what Madam Baba Yaga told you."

She who cleans up her own mess learns to not make it the next time.

Though Faybelle didn't want to admit it, she couldn't clean up this mess on her own. She needed to swallow her pride. She needed help.

Chapter 19

A Dark Confession

Madam Baba Yaga's office had spent the afternoon running through the Enchanted Forest, laying eggs, and was now resting on a hilltop above the school. With its chicken legs stretched out, the office snored gently and didn't stir, not even when Faybelle knocked on the door.

"Hello, Faybelle. I've been expecting you." The professor was sitting cross-legged on her pillow, floating in front of a crackling fire. Though it was stuffy in the office, she'd wrapped her scarf around

her shoulders and she wore a thick pair of wool socks. "Just warming up my old bones," she explained. "Come, have a seat."

Faybelle settled into a big, cushy chair. Despite the numerous patches, stuffing was leaking out. She arranged her cape. She felt ridiculous wearing it, but she still wanted to hide her injured wings. Once settled, she looked around the office. Like most professors, Madam Baba Yaga had an extensive collection of books, but she also had a crystal ball collection and a wall of framed degrees. A thin trail of smoke arose from a bowl of burning incense. Faybelle fidgeted. There was no use stalling. She'd come here for a reason. "You know everything, don't you? That's why you've been expecting me."

"I would never profess to knowing *everything*. But I am aware of certain magical happenings." Madam Baba Yaga motioned with her hand. A kettle that had been sitting on a grate over the fire drifted across the room and began to pour its contents into a mug. "Though tea is all the rage on campus these

days, I still prefer strong black coffee. Would you like a cup?"

"No, thank you." Faybelle fidgeted. It wasn't just the temperature of the room that was making her uncomfortable. It was also a jittery feeling in her stomach. Had coming here been a mistake? Should she leave and never tell anyone the truth? "I...I..."

"I'm listening."

"If I tell you why I'm here, will it go on my student record?"

The mug floated into Madam Baba Yaga's hand. She took a few sips. Her hoop earrings gleamed in the firelight. "Do you *want* this conversation to be recorded on your student record?"

"No! I don't want anyone to know what happened. I don't want to ruin my reputation."

After another sip, the professor set the mug onto her desk, then folded her hands in her lap. "Very well. For this meeting I shall remove my professor hat." She mimicked taking off a hat and casting it aside. "I am no longer acting as your teacher. Whatever you say shall be completely confidential." She paused. "Unless, of course, you broke a law. Did you break a law?" Faybelle shook her head. "Excellent. Proceed."

There was so much to say. Faybelle didn't know how to begin. "I made a huge mess," she blurted. Then the whole story poured out. How Justine asked the fairies to audition, how Faybelle wanted to play the part. How she went to the Vault of Lost Tales and found the wilted-wing spell. How she cheerhexed it, then hit herself with the spell, then found out that Cupid was also auditioning. How she shot Cupid's arrows and missed, and now her Cheerhexing Squad was all messed up, so they would have to forfeit their competition. And how Cupid would now get the part! "This kind of stuff isn't supposed to happen to me. I'm the daughter of the Dark Fairy. I should be good at dark magic." She sniffled. What was that? Were her eyes filling with tears? She turned away and wiped them with her sleeve.

"You might be interested to learn that many years ago, a student came to this very office and sat in that very same chair."

"I don't care about another—"

Madam Baba Yaga raised her hand. "Have patience, Ms. Thorn."

Faybelle sighed. "Sorry."

"As I was saying, this student came to me with a problem. She was auditioning for the lead in the school choir. Wanting to eliminate the competition, she tried to steal her rival's voice, but her attempt at dark magic was a failure. The only way she could tell me the truth was to write it on paper." She pointed at a filing cabinet. The third drawer opened, a file rose into the air, then a small slip of paper floated out. It flew toward Faybelle, who reached up and grabbed it. "Go on, Ms. Thorn. Read it."

> Dear Madam Baba Yaga,
> I made a terrible mistake. I cast a spell, but it bounced off a mirror, and now I've stolen my own voice. Can you help me?

Faybelle recognized the handwriting. "My mother?" It wasn't possible. Her mother would never make such a rookie mistake. Everyone knew not to cast spells near mirrors.

"Do you think you are the only one whose magic has gone awry?" Madam Baba Yaga asked.

"But she's the Dark Fairy. She *is* dark magic."

"She wasn't always the Dark Fairy. She was once a student, just like you—impatient, self-important, and sometimes *overachieving*."

Faybelle's tears had dried. She sat up straight. "Hold on, you just said 'overachieving' as if it were some sort of insult. I work hard. What's wrong with that?"

"There is nothing wrong with hard work, but if you try to be the best at everything, you risk becoming the best at nothing. You spread yourself as thin as a fairy wing." Madam Baba Yaga slid off the pillow and walked over to Faybelle. "President of the Villain Club, captain of the Cheerhexing Squad, a full course load, plus you're an honor roll student.

And now you want to be a lead in the upcoming theatrical production? Why?"

"It's the wicked fairy queen. I want the whole student body to see me in that role."

"They already see you in that role, Ms. Thorn. Haven't you noticed the way they look at you?" She took the paper from Faybelle and returned it to the filing cabinet. "Once your mother decided to focus on the things that really mattered to her, rather than on the activities she thought would make her *seem* important, she began to grow. Her magic began to grow. Magic is unpredictable and, thus, requires great focus. Anything that is worthwhile requires great focus." She closed the cabinet drawer, then turned her attention back to Faybelle. "Emotions are also unpredictable. Sometimes we can't control them. There is no shame in our emotions." She stared intently at Faybelle.

Faybelle frowned. "What are you talking about? What *emotions*?"

"I understand that you are feeling sorry *for your-self*. You have wilted wings, and that must be a terri-ble sensation. But is anything else troubling you?"

Faybelle folded her arms, her expression rigid with defiance. *Try to prove I'm feeling something. Go ahead.* But there was that lump in her throat again. And that heaviness in her chest. "You think I feel bad because I hurt other people? Other fairies?" She snorted. "I'm a villain. Of course I don't feel bad. If I did, that would mean I'm a total failure!" She relaxed her arms a bit. "Wouldn't it?"

Madam Baba Yaga did not respond.

"I suppose you want me to say that I'm sorry I hurt my cheerhexers. They didn't do anything to deserve wilted wings, and they certainly didn't want to be in love with Humphrey. And I suppose that Farrah, who's *so nice to everyone*, and who makes *dreams come true* with her magic"—Faybelle rolled her eyes—"I suppose she didn't deserve wilted wings, either. And maybe, just maybe, I feel a little bad. And maybe I wish I could go back in time and never cast that spell, but I can't do that. You said no more magic."

Still, Madam Baba Yaga said nothing.

Faybelle leaped to her feet. "Holy epic fairy failure!" She began to pace. "What's wrong with me? How can I be a villain if I feel sorry for my victims?"

"There's nothing wrong with you," Madam Baba Yaga assured her. "Villain status doesn't mean you are an emotionless robot. On the contrary. Fairies feel and sense everything at a deeper level than those without wings. A dark fairy is the most sensitive of all." The professor's old legs creaked as she walked toward Faybelle. She clasped both her hands around Faybelle's. "Savor this lesson, my child. Use dark magic only when absolutely necessary. In this case, it was not needed."

"You think I would have gotten the role without magic?"

Madam Baba Yaga nodded. "Who better to play a wicked fairy queen than you? Justine knows that."

A clock chimed. The office began to tremble as it rose up on its chicken legs. "It's time for some exercise, which means we will soon be on the move," Madam Baba Yaga said. "Perhaps this is a good time for you to make your exit."

Faybelle certainly didn't want to get stuck running around the Enchanted Forest with the professor's weird office. "Madam, you said I needed to clean up my own messes. Is there a spell I can use to undo my magic?"

"All dark fairies have the power to undo their magic, but there's a catch."

Faybelle groaned. "What?"

"The spell will work on your victims, but it won't work on you. Your wings will have to recover on their own."

"I figured you were going to say that."

Pyramid

Perfection

With special permission from Madam Baba Yaga, Faybelle cheerhexed a spell to reverse all the magical chaos she'd created over the last couple of days. She chose to perform it on the athletic field—the one place where a cheer wouldn't raise suspicions. There weren't many students around—just the Ever After High Croquet Team, and they were on the far side of the field with their hedgehogs and mallets.

Magic, magic, hear my cry. (stomp)
Dark deeds, dark deeds,
say bye-bye. (stomp)
Magic, magic, in your face. (clap)
Erase it all,
without a trace. (stomp)

As the fairy dust cleared, and she lowered her pom-poms, there was a long stretch of not knowing. Had it worked? Or had she, the daughter of the Dark Fairy, once again failed to achieve her magical goals?

Then, on the horizon, six figures appeared—in flight. A shiver darted up Faybelle's spine, for it was a spelltacular sight to behold. But, alas, even as the six fairies soared and dipped, her own wings hung against her back, as wilted as forgotten flowers.

"Our wings work!" they exclaimed as they landed beside her. They began to bounce up and down like, well, like cheerhexers.

"But weren't we chasing someone?"

"I'm not sure."

"You were chasing Humphrey."

"We were?"

"Oh my godmother, how embarrassing!"

These were all good signs. Not only did their wings work, but they'd also clearly gotten over Humphrey. No lovesickness meant they were no longer under a spell and would be ready to practice. Things could get back to normal. Except for Faybelle, who was still under a curse.

But there was no time to wallow in self-pity. She hexted the team for an emergency practice session.

"Hurry up!" she called as Hunter, Nina, and Holly ran onto the field. "What took you so long?"

"I was getting a trim at the Tower Salon," Holly said, though this wasn't obvious, because her hair still hung to her knees.

Nina was carrying an armful of books. "I was studying for my Environmental Magic exam," she explained.

An ax was slung over Hunter's brawny shoulder.

"And I was chopping wood for Hagatha's new wood-fired pizza oven."

Because Faybelle couldn't hover, she stepped up onto a bench to ensure that her teammates could see her. "The team is back to normal, so we don't have to forfeit after all. I think we can still master the inverted pyramid, but we have to make up for lost time." She put her hands on her hips. "Where's Farrah?"

"Here I am!" Half flying, half skipping, the blue-haired fairy waved as she approached. "My wings are back to normal! They're not sick anymore. Justine is going to let me audition." Though this did not surprise Faybelle, it still stung. So much effort for what?

"That's great," Holly and Nina said as they hugged her. But when Farrah looked at Faybelle, her smile vanished.

"What about *your* wings?" Farrah asked.

Faybelle untied the cape and let it fall onto the bench. She didn't need to hide her wings. The fact that they still hung lifeless was as clear as the Ever

After High sky. Despite her condition, she'd muster some pride! "Apparently, dark fairies have such a complex wing structure it takes longer for them to heal." She raised an eyebrow, daring anyone to argue with that obvious fact. No one did. She clapped her hands. "Okay, enough chitchat. We have work to do. Let's practice our cheer for regionals."

Everyone grabbed pom-poms. Then, chanting the cheer Faybelle had written, they performed their pivots, turns, and kicks in perfect sync.

Spell!
Say what? Say what?
Spell!
That's what we do!
We spell,
We spell for you!

The final grand move, the one that would blow the audience away, was the inverted pyramid. At least, that was the plan. With looks of trepidation, Hunter took his place. Then, with a boost from the rest of the

team, Holly and Nina balanced on Hunter's shoulders, forming the second row.

"Looking good," Faybelle said. "Next row."

Two of the fairies flew and landed carefully on the outside shoulders of the second row. Farrah then flew and landed gently, one foot on Nina's inside shoulder, one foot on Holly's inside shoulder. There was some wobbling.

"She's stepping on my hair," Holly complained.

"Steady," Faybelle said. "Focus." One of the fairies elbowed Farrah. "Hocus focus! How are you doing, Hunter?"

His face was turning red. "I'm okay. Just hurry it up. I can't do this much longer!"

As soon as the three rows were steady, she called for the next row.

The last four fairies took to the air, then gently landed on the shoulders of the third row. Farrah's knees buckled, but only for a moment. Nina began to sag. Faybelle clenched her jaw. They were so close.

Faybelle held her breath. The pyramid teetered to the right, then the left.

"Whoa," Hunter moaned.

"I can't hold on any longer," Nina warned.

"Anything that is worthwhile requires great focus," Faybelle told them, quoting her wise old professor. "Close your eyes and think of nothing but this pyramid."

As her team followed their captain's instructions, the inverted pyramid took its perfect upside-down shape.

Faybelle gave them a standing ovation. The trophy would be theirs!

One by one, the fairies alighted, and the team gathered for a group cheer.

> *Stomp* (stomp, stomp), *stomp your feet!*
> *Ever After High* (clap) *can't be beat!*

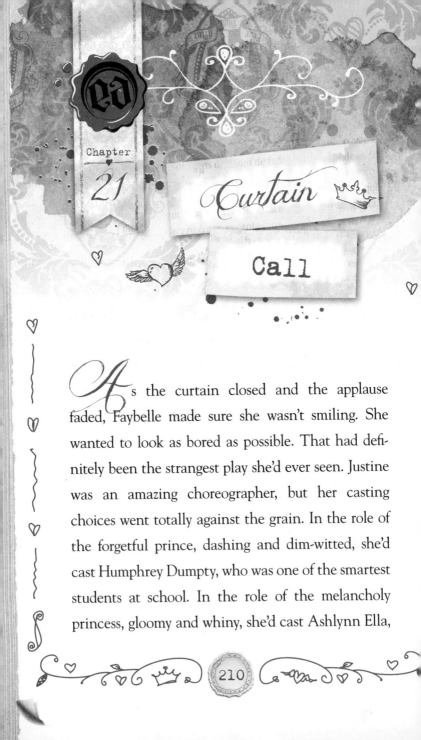

As the curtain closed and the applause faded, Faybelle made sure she wasn't smiling. She wanted to look as bored as possible. That had definitely been the strangest play she'd ever seen. Justine was an amazing choreographer, but her casting choices went totally against the grain. In the role of the forgetful prince, dashing and dim-witted, she'd cast Humphrey Dumpty, who was one of the smartest students at school. In the role of the melancholy princess, gloomy and whiny, she'd cast Ashlynn Ella,

who was always smiling and happy. And for the wicked fairy queen, brooding and evil, she'd cast Farrah Goodfairy, who was as twinkly and kind as a fairy could be. *Hello? Talk about an insult to dark fairies everywhere!*

But despite the unusual casting decisions, the play had been entertaining. Especially Humphrey's fight scene. He'd tripped over his own feet and almost impaled himself on his own stage sword. Having impaled herself with her own magic, Faybelle knew exactly how Humphrey felt. But the music had been good, and there'd been quite a few laughs. Cupid had landed a part in the chorus and had ended up with a mini solo.

"Wake up," Faybelle told her cheerhexers. All six of them had fallen asleep in the middle of the melancholy princess's monologue. "It's over."

"You would have been so much better," one of them said with a yawn.

"So much better."

"That little Goodfairy stank."

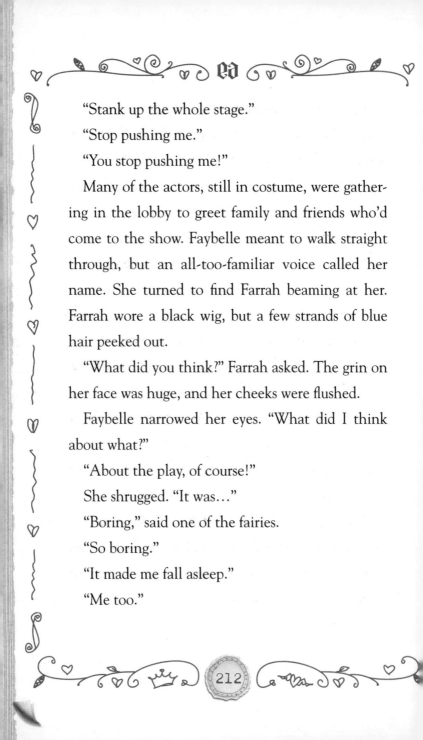

"Stank up the whole stage."

"Stop pushing me."

"You stop pushing me!"

Many of the actors, still in costume, were gathering in the lobby to greet family and friends who'd come to the show. Faybelle meant to walk straight through, but an all-too-familiar voice called her name. She turned to find Farrah beaming at her. Farrah wore a black wig, but a few strands of blue hair peeked out.

"What did you think?" Farrah asked. The grin on her face was huge, and her cheeks were flushed.

Faybelle narrowed her eyes. "What did I think about what?"

"About the play, of course!"

She shrugged. "It was…"

"Boring," said one of the fairies.

"So boring."

"It made me fall asleep."

"Me too."

"Oh, is that Humphrey? Hi, Humphrey!"

Faybelle raised a hand to quiet them. "The play was better than I hexpected," she said. If the Good-fairy wanted a bigger compliment than that, she'd have to stand there until Wonderland froze over.

"Oh, that's so nice to hear," Farrah said. Then her smile faded. "But the only reason I got the part was because your wings didn't heal in time. I feel so badly about that."

Faybelle didn't want to have this conversation. There was no time in her schedule to dwell on what might have been. "Look, you did fine. Even if my wings had healed in time, I'd already decided that I needed to cut back on my activities and focus on the things that are most important to me. *Acting* isn't one of those things."

"That sounds like a smart plan." Farrah's blue eyes twinkled. She stepped closer and lowered her voice. "But you and I both know the wicked fairy queen should have been your part."

The six fairies waited for Faybelle's response. Everyone in earshot turned and watched. Faybelle's wings shuddered. Of course the part should have been hers, but that was in the past. Faybelle was determined to be the sort of fairy who looked to the future. She wasn't going to fret about the fact that she'd messed up. After all, another very famous dark fairy had made youthful mistakes, too, and she'd turned out amazing! And Faybelle had also decided that she wasn't going to worry so much about whether everyone saw her the way she wanted them to see her. Her destiny had been decided, and she'd claim it when the time was right.

Farrah was still looking at her. "I'm sorry you didn't get the part."

"Sorry?" Faybelle threw back her head and laughed as deviously as she could. "Don't worry your pretty little self about me, Farrah Goodfairy. I get to play the part of the wicked fairy queen for the rest of my life." With dramatic flair, Faybelle unfurled her magnificent wings. The six cheerhexers cheered.

Everyone stepped aside. Was that fear she saw in a few eyes? *How delightful.*

Then she flew from the lobby.

And the air embraced her once again.

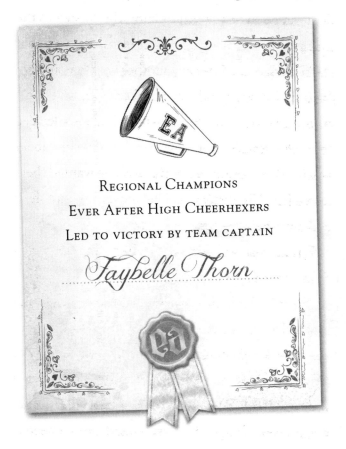

REGIONAL CHAMPIONS
EVER AFTER HIGH CHEERHEXERS
LED TO VICTORY BY TEAM CAPTAIN

Faybelle Thorn

ACKNOWLEDGMENTS

Once again, I am indebted to an amazing team of creative people, without whom this book would simply not be. In Gotham City, you will find my editors, Kara Sargent and Rachel Poloski, who guide and protect me. My brilliant copyeditor, Christine Ma, publicist extraordinaire Kristina Aven, and many more people, all an important part of the effort, listed here in no particular order (drumroll please): Mara Lander, Véronique Sweet, Annie McDonnell, Christina Quintero, Victoria Stapleton, and Andrew Smith.

And on the other coast, in La La Land, you will find the other half of the team, the geniuses behind the Ever After High brand, who provide me with fun new characters and the freedom to play around in their hilarious universe. Thank you to Ryan Ferguson, Debra Mostow Zakarin, Nicole Corse, Charnita Belcher, Stuart Smith, Sammie Suchland, Karen Painter, Kristine Lombardi, Robert Rudman, Talia Rodgers, Eric Vexelman, Lara Dalian, Audu Paden, Gary Leynes, and Izzy Garr.

Michael Bourret, I hope to continue this writing journey together forever after. And to Isabelle, Walker, and Bob, you are the wind beneath my fairy wings.

ABOUT THE AUTHOR

Suzanne Selfors feels like a Royal on some days and a Rebel on others. She's written many books for kids, including the Smells Like Dog series and the Imaginary Veterinary series.

She has two charming children and lives in a magical island kingdom, where she hopes it is her destiny to write stories forever after.